W9-AVH-758

THE UNWRITTEN GIRL

THE
UNWRITTEN GIRL

James Bow

A BOARDWALK BOOK
A MEMBER OF THE DUNDURN GROUP
TORONTO

Copyright © James Bow, 2006

All rights reserved. No part of this publication may be reproduced, stored in a retrieval system, or transmitted in any form or by any means, electronic, mechanical, photocopying, recording, or otherwise (except for brief passages for purposes of review) without the prior permission of Dundurn Press. Permission to photocopy should be requested from Access Copyright.

Editor: Barry Jowett
Copy-Editor: Andrea Waters
Design: Andrew Roberts
Printer: Webcom

Library and Archives Canada Cataloguing in Publication

Bow, James, 1972-
        The unwritten girl / James Bow.

ISBN-10: 1-55002-604-6
ISBN-13: 978-1-55002-604-7

I. Title.

PS8603.O973U97 2006   jC813'.6   C2006-900522-2

1   2   3   4   5   10   09   08   07   06

  Canada

We acknowledge the support of the Canada Council for the Arts and the Ontario Arts Council for our publishing program. We also acknowledge the financial support of the Government of Canada through the Book Publishing Industry Development Program and The Association for the Export of Canadian Books, and the Government of Ontario through the Ontario Book Publishers Tax Credit program, and the Ontario Media Development Corporation.

Care has been taken to trace the ownership of copyright material used in this book. The author and the publisher welcome any information enabling them to rectify any references or credits in subsequent editions.

J. Kirk Howard, President

Printed and bound in Canada.
Printed on recycled paper.

www.dundurn.com

Dundurn Press
3 Church Street, Suite 500
Toronto, Ontario, Canada
M5E 1M2

Gazelle Book Services Limited
White Cross Mills
High Town, Lancaster, England
LA1 4XS

Dundurn Press
2250 Military Road
Tonawanda, NY
U.S.A. 14150

THE UNWRITTEN GIRL

DEDICATION

You know who you are.

PROLOGUE

Rosemary read.

* * *

Marjorie gasped. "What is this place?"

She stood, with her brother, John, and her new friend Andrew, at the base of the tallest, largest building they had ever seen. Chrome jaguars guarded the steps, frozen in mid-leap. The other buildings seemed to crowd together, pushing them up the stairs. A thousand Zeppelins patrolled the sky.

"Is this where the people went?" asked Marjorie.

"Yes," said the Sentinel.

"That's comforting," deadpanned Andrew. "I think we should go now."

"Perhaps there was some disaster," said John. "I wonder what happened here; it's like the *Marie Celeste*!"

"Do you wish to see the people?" The Sentinel, moving stiffly on stone joints, stepped past them and pushed open the doors.

"That walking statue is just so creepy," said Andrew. He put his hand on Marjorie's shoulder. "Let's get out of here!"

"No." Marjorie pushed her horn-rimmed glasses further up on her nose. "I want to see."

The Sentinel ushered them forward.

They found themselves in a vast, dark cathedral. Huge marble slabs stood suspended from the ceiling, row upon row, seven feet wide and tall, and two feet thick. Some swung almost imperceptibly, as if something inside them stirred.

The rhythmic heartbeat of the city hammered off the walls, breaking their thoughts to well-ordered pieces.

"But ... where are all the people?" asked Marjorie.

John looked up at the slabs. His face went white. "Marjorie ..."

The doors slammed behind them.

* * *

Rosemary winced. She turned the page.

***

Each slab held the impression of a person: here an old man with wide staring eyes, there a young woman, a child; each as different as people are from one another.

Frightened but curious, Marjorie led the way onto a moving sidewalk towards a second set of giant doors. The Sentinel pressed Andrew and John to follow her. "Ours is a powerful civilization," he said. "We have built many wonders. But civilizations grow old, and old civilizations disappear. Knowing this, the people of this planet built the great Machine. The Machine was the pinnacle of our technology, capable of answering any question put to it and performing any action asked of it. We told it our fears and we asked it to preserve us so that our civilization would never die."

"But I don't understand," said Andrew. "Where are all the people?"

"The Machine did as the people instructed," said the Sentinel. "It automated all the processes and turned all the people into stone."

The second set of doors swung open as they approached, and the heartbeat intensified. At the end of a long hall sat the Machine.

***

Rosemary swallowed hard. She flipped ahead.

***

Metal claws snaked down from the ceiling and grabbed their wrists and ankles.

The Sentinel spread its arms as if puzzled. "Why do you resist? The Machine preserves all on this planet. You are on this planet, so you must be preserved."

"We've got to get out of here!" Andrew yelled.

"Concentrate, Marjorie!" shouted John. "Teleport now!"

"I can't!" cried Marjorie. "It's the Machine! It's breaking my thoughts!"

Andrew screamed as the metal pincers wrenched him off his feet.

"Marjorie, do something!" John shouted as the claws pulled him away. There was the sound of clanging metal, the hiss of steam. Her brother's yells ended abruptly.

"Andrew! John!" Marjorie screamed. She struggled vainly against the metal cables wrapping around her body, pulling her to the Machine. "No!"

***

Horrified, Rosemary threw the book across her room.

It landed with a thud, and Marjorie's story slammed shut.

CHAPTER ONE

THE GIRL WHO FOLDED HERSELF

"What if we could travel at the speed of thought?"
— Marjorie Campbell

Rosemary Watson slapped her schoolbooks down on a study cubicle. The Outsiders *has to be the most depressing book ever*, she thought. She pushed her fingers beneath her thick glasses and rubbed the bridge of her nose.

The school bus was late and getting later. Through the window behind her came muffled laughter and the smack of icy snowballs. Rosemary sighed and slumped in her seat.

"Really, Rosemary," said a voice behind her. "You would think someone as bookish as you would appreciate good literature!"

She whirled around. Benson sat twisted in his seat by the study cubicle behind her, grinning.

"Go away," she snapped.

"What's the matter, Sage?" said Benson. "'Fraid of a little snow?"

"Don't you have homework?" said Rosemary.

The school librarian shushed them. They looked up and caught her grim look. Benson flashed Rosemary a cheeky grin and turned back to his books.

Rosemary turned away. Benson had been imitating what Mr. Reed, her English teacher, had said when he'd discovered she was a chapter behind in her assigned reading of *The Outsiders*. The class, of course, had laughed. She hadn't bothered to explain. She'd sat silently in her seat, her face red, feeling as though a spotlight were on her.

It had been a bad day, and her classmates weren't about to let it end, not while everyone waited for the school buses after the first snowfall of the season. So instead of standing in the schoolyard with an invisible target pinned to her forehead, she had chosen to hide in the library, taking refuge in the *Encyclopedia Britannica*.

The school library was half the size of the public library her father managed, but at least it had encyclopedias and the smell of paper. She felt the stress of the day seeping out amongst the hushed tomes and the facts and figures. She took a deep breath and smiled.

Then she coughed. The scent of old paper was suddenly more powerful and tinged with mildew. It clung to her like cobwebs.

Rosemary stood up and looked around. The smell seemed to be coming from one of the fiction aisles. She slipped past racks of battered paperbacks and stepped into the stacks.

A burnt-out light cast the aisle in shadow, and the shelves towered over her like a hedge maze. A girl stood where the shelves met the wall. She was flipping through a book. There was something odd about her.

Rosemary pushed her glasses further up on her nose for a better look.

The girl looked a lot like Rosemary. She was about the same age, wore glasses, and had shoulder-length brown hair. She wore a school uniform, though, and that was what made her look odd. Rosemary's school didn't have uniforms, and more than that, the cut of the girl's clothes was out of date. Her glasses were horn-rimmed instead of round. It was as though she had stepped out of the 1950s, or Rosemary had stepped in.

The girl stopped paging, then turned and looked at Rosemary. Their eyes locked. The girl's eyes were not friendly.

"Who —" Rosemary stammered. "What's wrong?"

The girl turned towards Rosemary and disappeared.

Rosemary jumped back. The girl had not faded into nothingness, as though she were a ghost. A ghost Rosemary could handle, maybe. Instead, she had folded out of existence, growing thinner as she turned until she was a line and then nothing at all, as though she were a piece of paper. Rosemary goggled at the empty space, and she swore it was looking back at her.

The smell of dust was so intense, Rosemary thought her throat would close. She choked.

A hand fell on her shoulder. Rosemary gasped and whirled around.

Behind her was a tall boy with a flop of light brown hair, a lot of freckles, and eyes that looked friendly, or maybe sad. He smiled at her. "Hey!"

She struggled a moment to place him, then remembered him: the new kid in English class, off to one side, neither perched near the front of the class nor hiding in the back. When the rest of the class had laughed at her, he hadn't joined in. "You're ..." she began.

The boy grinned ruefully and recited, "Peter. Peter McAllister, the new kid. From Toronto. The school buses are here." He slung his backpack over his shoulder. Benson was already checking his books out.

She looked back at the aisle. The sense of being watched by empty space returned. She tried to steady her breath.

"What's wrong?" said Peter. "You see something?"

She took a step back and turned away. "It's nothing," she said. *It's nothing*, she thought. *Don't act crazy*. Leaving Peter behind, she grabbed up her backpack and her winter coat and ran for the door.

The blast of cold air blanched Rosemary's cheeks, but that was not why she staggered to a stop outside the entrance to Clarksbury Junior High. Across the yard, she could hear the shouts of the children heading towards the school buses, but around her it was too quiet. She could hear the whistle of the wind. The low walls nearby seemed to be giggling.

She judged the distance between herself and the school buses, calculated how long it would take for her to run, then nixed that idea. Never let them see you run.

The door swung open, and Peter stepped out with Benson. Peter gave her a smile as he passed. Rosemary shouldered her backpack, pushed her glasses further up on her nose, focused on the nearest school bus, and strode forward.

For several steps, nothing happened. Then, as she got out into the open, somebody shouted, "Get her!" Kids leapt out of cover, and the air became alive with snowballs. They caught Peter as well as Rosemary. He laughed and scooped up snowballs of his own, returning fire. Then Rosemary yelled as an incoming shot caught her on the ear and sent her glasses flying.

She waved her hands at the blurry white onslaught. "Stop! Stop, you idiots! I've lost my glasses!"

The volley stopped. Rosemary clawed snow from her eyes and sank to her knees to paw at the ground.

There were chuckles from the crowd. Peter dropped the snowball he was holding. "Hey, are you okay?"

Rosemary couldn't stop her angry, rasping breaths. She would *not* cry. "Just help me look!"

"Looking for these?" A shape pressed forward and picked up something off the snow. Rosemary froze. She recognized the voice of Leo Cameron, noted schoolyard bully. *Great*, she thought. *First* The Outsiders, *then folding people, and now this.*

"Give them to me," she growled.

Leo chuckled. "Now, now, Sage, ask nice!"

"Come on, Leo," said Benson. "Go easy on her."

"Yeah, don't make her crazy like her brother," shouted someone from the crowd. There was a ripple of laughter.

Rosemary shot up from her hands and knees. Her breathing quickened. Her eyes glistened. Then she let out a yell and charged, arms swinging. Leo ducked back, and she spun herself around and landed heavily in the snow. Leo laughed. "Where're your manners, Sage? Say please!"

Peter pushed forward and stood chest to chest with Leo, looking down. He stuck out his hand. "Please."

There was a pause as everyone stood poised, waiting for something to happen. In her blurred vision, Rosemary saw Peter, tall, towering over the bullies, and for a minute she thought of her brother, Theo.

Finally, Leo tossed the glasses to Rosemary. They hit her chest and she caught them. "Go ahead and have your glasses; like I care. C'mon, guys!"

His friends filed after him, followed by the rest of the crowd. Peter stayed close while Rosemary smeared her glasses with her scarf.

"Thanks," she said, bitterly. Almost as bad as being teased was being rescued from it. Almost. She put her glasses on again.

Peter handed over her fallen hat. "You've got a nice left hook."

Rosemary flushed and looked away. "I lost my temper."

"Better than just standing there. You're Rosemary, right? Rosemary Watson?"

Her eyes narrowed. "*You* know *me*?"

He shrugged. "I see you get on the bus every day. I live just down the road."

There was a pause. The two stared at each other. "So ..." Rosemary began.

Then there was the sound of engines. Rosemary whirled and charged across the snow. "Wait! Hey!" But the buses pulled into the street, turned a corner, and were gone. She stumbled to a stop and threw up her hands.

Peter caught up with her, puffing. "I'm sorry! I forgot they were about to leave."

She sighed. "It's okay; my fault. Perfect ending to a perfect day. I'll walk." She turned to him, nodding curtly. "Thanks for the help. See you Monday." And she turned away and trudged off.

A moment later, she heard the scuff of snow behind her. "Why do they call you 'Sage'?"

She froze. "Are you following me?"

"Do you mind?" He had his hands in his pockets and his shoulders hunched. He smiled at her sheepishly. "It's a long way, and we live on the same street."

She considered a moment, then shrugged. "Whatever. Free country."

They walked through the main street of Clarksbury, passing fish and tackle shops closed for the season and a single, quiet convenience store. The proprietor of Luigi's Pizzeria and Bait Shop looked up from the scrape of his shovel and waved to them as they passed; Rosemary took no notice. On the road, a single car breezed by.

"So, why *do* they call you Sage?" asked Peter.

She hunched forward. "My family called me Sage. My brother let it slip. It stuck."

"Your family calls you Sage?"

"Because I read encyclopedias," she replied. "It was okay when they did it."

"'Parsley, sage, rosemary, and thyme.' That's a folk song, isn't it?"

"How would I know? I don't sing!"

"Leo probably doesn't either. He sounds like a cat with a hairball."

Rosemary snorted.

They neared the edge of town. Their boots squelched on slush as the sidewalk gave way to gravel. The houses receded, and the Niagara Escarpment, a one-hundred-foot rise of rock and trees that surrounded Clarksbury on three sides, drew closer. They turned at a sign pointing to a road that broke off the main highway and ascended the Escarpment. "45th Parallel Road," it said, with a sign beneath boasting, "Halfway between pole and equator."

Peter puffed as they trudged up the slope. "Well, not much further, Sage."

She rounded on him. Her fists clenched. "What did you call me?"

"S-Sage," he said, swallowing. "Do you mind?" He raised his hands. "Look, I won't say it like they mean it, but like your brother meant it and stuff. It's a good nickname; it means 'wise one.'"

She looked at him. "You always quote dictionaries?"

He shrugged. "Got a problem with that?" He gave her a grin.

She rolled her eyes. "And it's me they tease." She looked over his shoulder. "Uh-oh. A squall's coming in."

He looked back. Behind them, the slate expanse of Georgian Bay swept out to piled black clouds on the horizon. A white chop was developing on the dark water. "What's a squall? A snowstorm or something?"

"You'll find out if we don't hurry." She turned up the slope.

The squall overtook them before they'd gone half a mile, starting with a few flecks and a short gust of wind pressing at their backs. As they topped the Escarpment, the world disappeared into whirling snow and icy daggers slipped under their collars. The slush turned crunchy. Rosemary stumbled, and Peter hauled her up. She stared at his hand in hers, then shook it off. Then a gust nearly knocked them off their feet. Rosemary grabbed Peter's hand and ploughed forward. Finally, they came to the Watsons' mailbox and leaned on it, gasping. "I wish we hadn't missed the bus," Rosemary wheezed.

"I don't." Peter gave her a smile. It looked wistful. "Well, I guess I'd better get going." He turned to leave.

She stopped him. "What are you doing?"

"Going home."

"In this weather?"

He raised an eyebrow with small smile. "Where else would I go?"

The wind blew snow into her mouth and she spluttered.

Behind them, a screen door banged open and a man shouted, "Rosemary! Come inside, for heaven's sake!"

They stumbled along a pathway and up swayback steps to an old stone house. The wind blew them past a front door plastered with snow. They entered a room lined with bookcases. The house smelled deliciously of spicy tomato sauce.

A German shepherd ploughed into Rosemary, knocking her down, and started licking her face, despite her muffled protests. Then it looked up at Peter and growled.

"Shamus!" Rosemary grabbed her dog. "No! Friend! Peter's a friend!"

Shamus stopped growling, sniffed Peter's leg, barked once, and then trotted off. Peter swallowed.

"He approves of you," said Rosemary.

Rosemary's father came back from the kitchen, wearing glasses, a "Kiss the Cook" apron, two potholders shaped like pig puppets, and a scowl. "Young lady! Why didn't you call me for a lift? The radio has been going on all afternoon about this weather!"

"I'm sorry, Dad!" Rosemary pulled off her coat and boots. "I didn't know about the weather. I walked home with —" She hesitated, hardly believing she was doing this. "Peter."

Rosemary's father pushed his glasses further up on his nose and peered at Peter. Then he snatched off his potholders and extended his hand. "I'm sorry! This is hardly a proper welcome. You live up the road, don't you?"

"Yes, sir. Peter McAllister."

"I'm Alexander Watson, Rosemary's father." Mr. Watson shook Peter's hand and smiled brightly, all trace of his anger gone. "Come in! It's not often Rosemary brings home gentlemen callers. In fact, I think this is a first. May I ask what your intentions are towards my daughter?"

"Dad!" Rosemary flushed red. Peter kept his eyes on the floor and didn't say anything.

Rosemary's father chuckled and patted Peter on the back. He nodded over his shoulder. "The phone's in the kitchen. You'd better give your father a call; dinner's almost ready."

"He's my uncle, actually," said Peter, pulling off his coat and heading for the phone. He jumped back as a small blonde girl bounded down the stairs, holding a Lego model aloft and making engine noises.

Mr. Watson cleared his throat. "Trisha, no landing airplanes in the kitchen."

The girl made a graceful turn and flew back up the stairs.

"Trish," Rosemary explained to Peter as she passed.

In the kitchen, Mr. Watson lifted the lid off a steaming pot. "Rosemary, could you and Peter set the table? Your mother and Theo should be home soon."

Rosemary nudged Peter as he hung up the phone. "Come on, I'll show you where the placemats are."

As he followed her into the dining room, rich and dark after the bright kitchen, she added, "Sorry about my dad. He likes to tease everybody. It's his way of making people feel welcome."

"I didn't mind," said Peter. He looked around. Bookshelves lined the walls like wainscotting.

Rosemary glanced at the table and sighed. "Dad forgot to put the plates out again."

She pulled up a chair and climbed up to reach the top of a tall Victorian cabinet full of plates, linens, and a shelf of cookbooks. Grabbing what she needed, she hopped down and bumped into Peter, who'd had his arm out to steady her. She frowned at him a moment, then passed him the plates.

They circled the table, laying out mismatched china and an assortment of cutlery. Rosemary asked, "You live with your uncle?"

Peter looked away. "Um ... yeah."

"Your parents are ..."

He shifted on his feet. "They died in a car accident when I was nine."

Rosemary set a plate down with a thump. "Oh, I'm sorry!"

Peter coughed. "It — it's nothing. It was years ago."

"But you only just got here."

"I bounced around foster homes for a while before the province allowed my uncle to take me in. Something about my parents not having a will or something saying who'd take care of me after —" He took a deep breath, then grinned at her. "Anyway, it's over now. I'm with my uncle, whisked away from downtown Toronto to greater Clarksbury."

"I'm sorry," said Rosemary again. "What a thing to bring up."

"Don't worry," said Peter. "I'm looking forward to dinner. I like my uncle, but ... well ... it's just him and me in that place and he doesn't believe in suppertime. He buys things you heat up in the microwave. You have a real family, Sage." He grinned at her.

She looked away. "Hardly normal, though."

"I wouldn't wish normal on my worst enemy," said Peter. "But I see what you mean. I've never seen so many books outside of a library. And where's your television set?"

Rosemary grimaced. "Mom won't have one in the house."

Peter raised an eyebrow. "Explains your love of books."

Rosemary looked up at him. His smile was perfectly benign. No teasing here. "Partly," she said at last. "Dad's the other reason."

"The other reason for what?" Mr. Watson set a steaming bowl of spaghetti on the table. He took off his pig-puppet potholders and untied his apron.

"We were talking about the books," said Peter.

Mr. Watson laughed. "Oh, yes. Town librarian isn't a job; it's a way of life. My love of books doesn't turn off when I get home." He glanced at a clock on the wall in the shape of a cat, its tail a pendulum. "Listen, kids, I think we'd better dig in before dinner gets cold."

"But what about Mom and Theo?" asked Rosemary.

"Your mom's already two hours late from picking up Theo."

Peter nudged Rosemary. "Is Theo your brother?"

"Yeah," she said. "He's studying English at the University of Toronto."

"The storm may have slowed them down," Mr. Watson continued. "Waiting for them is likely to leave dinner cold, so let's eat. Just make sure you leave enough for them to warm up in the microwave."

After dinner, Mr. Watson led Peter on a tour of the house. "Books, books, books!" said Peter, staring up the main staircase and the shelves lining one wall of it. "How did you get so many?"

"Forty years of shopping in used book stores," Mr. Watson replied.

"Have you read them all?" Peter asked Rosemary.

She snorted. "No!"

"I haven't read them all, either," said Mr. Watson. "Almost as intense as the joy of reading is the joy of just having a book. They may be able to put books on the computer these days, but it's not the same." He pulled out a thick tome with a dust jacket: *All The Strange Hours* by Loren C. Eiseley. "Here, feel the weight! Feel the quality of the paper!"

"I read it," said Rosemary brightly.

Peter flipped through the pages and looked at her with a raised eyebrow. "This is a book about geology."

"Rosemary is an avid reader of science books," said Mr. Watson. "I hardly ever see her in the fiction section. Which reminds me: Did you remember to bring your English homework home this time, Rosemary?"

She drooped. "Yes, Dad."

"What is it?"

"Another two chapters of *The Outsiders*."

Peter studied her face. "What's wrong with *The Outsiders*?"

"Only that it's the grimmest book on the planet!"

Peter chuckled. "Wait until they make you read *That Was Then, This is Now*. Talk about dreary."

Mr. Watson laughed. "I once heard Ms. Hinton say that the ending of *That Was Then, This is Now* made readers throw the book against the wall. She seemed rather proud of that. But be that as it may, Rosemary, if two chapters of Hinton have been assigned, then two chapters shall be read."

She sighed. "I can't read *A Midsummer Night's Dream* again?"

"You don't get credit for reading the same book over again. Come on, Rosemary, you've got to build an appreciation for good literature."

"Why do people have to die to make it good literature?"

He blinked at her, then mussed her hair. "It's not always like that."

"It's like that a lot!"

Just then, they saw lights turn into their driveway. Rosemary brightened. "Mom's home!"

They ran for the door. Shamus beat them to it, his tail banging into an umbrella stand. Then he stopped. He whimpered once and shied away.

Rosemary frowned. "Shamus, what's wr—"

Mr. Watson yanked open the front door. The squall had broken, but snow was still falling. Two figures stood on either side of a station wagon, recognizable even as silhouettes.

Rosemary's mother darted towards her husband. "Alex!"

"Kate," said Mr. Watson. "Kate, what's wrong?"

"It's Theo!" said Kate Watson. "Alex, there's something wrong with Theo!"

CHAPTER TWO

BEHIND THE SHELF

"That's how it started. That's how it went until she stopped."
— Marjorie Campbell

Theo walked past his parents, his attention captured by a book in his hands, a paperback with a painting of a book on the cover. "Mom, I'm okay," he said, without looking at her. He moved like someone half in another world: a sleepwalker, or a scuba diver, or someone in a lot of pain.

Mr. Watson, his breath fogging, touched his son's arm. "Theo?"

Theo paused. He turned. He focused. "Hello," he said. Then he stepped into the house. They followed him in.

"He's been like that ever since I saw him in his residence," said Rosemary's mother. "I found him staring into that book, and I had to shout to get him to acknowledge me. It's like he has tardive dyskinesia — flat affect."

Peter blinked. "Huh?"

Rosemary tugged at Theo's sleeve. "Theo?"

Theo gave her a smile, but his eyes were vacant. "Hello, Rosie," he said. Then he turned back to his paperback book. Rosemary frowned at it, tried to see if there was a title. She caught sight only of an image of smoke emanating from an open book before he walked away, into the kitchen.

"Drugs?" Mr. Watson blanched.

"No," said Rosemary's mother. "I took him to the hospital. That's why I was late. I had them run toxicology tests. Physically, he's fine, but I don't know, Alex, I don't know. Who's he?" She stared at Peter.

"Rosemary's friend," said Mr. Watson.

"Rosemary brought home a boy?"

Rosemary huffed. "He's just a friend!"

Peter shifted on his feet. "The squall's let up a bit. Maybe I should go home?"

"I'll drive you," said Mr. Watson. "Let's get our coats on."

Rosemary stood in the living room, torn between Peter and her father preparing to leave and her brother in the kitchen. After a moment, she settled on her brother, but froze at the kitchen door. Theo stood, facing the refrigerator, staring at the jumble of coloured-letter magnets as if he expected them to change and spell something. Her mother stood behind him, still in her winter coat.

I'm not supposed to be here yet, Rosemary thought, and she turned back to the living room.

Peter and her father were ready for winter and stepping out the door. Rosemary stopped Peter in the foyer. "Wait!" She clasped his hand in a sort of handshake. "Thanks for rescuing me." She pulled a face.

"I wasn't rescuing you, I was rescuing Leo."

She scowled at him. Then her mouth quirked. She snorted and broke out into a grin.

He smiled at her. After a moment, she sobered. "Thanks," she said again. "I guess ... see you Monday."

"Yeah, at school," he said. "Not much to do till then. You doing anything this weekend?"

She started. "I'm ... I'm working!"

"You work? Where?"

"At the library. I volunteer."

"Isn't the library closed on Sunday?"

Rosemary spluttered. Mr. Watson called from the idling car. "Ready?"

Peter nodded. Then he turned back to her. "Your brother's going to be okay."

She looked away. "How would you know?"

"I've seen worse."

He turned away, leaving her staring, and got into the car. A moment later, the station wagon pulled out of the driveway and onto the snow-covered road. It crept carefully into the distance.

Rosemary stared after it for a few seconds, then closed the front door. She started for the kitchen, but hearing her mother's calm, measured tones that Rosemary knew were a few steps away from breaking, she hesitated. Then she went to the closet, pulled on her boots, coat, and hat, and went outside.

Her father had made a rink in the backyard with a garden hose. The ice was covered with new snow, but Rosemary was able to entertain herself with running slides. Her mind went over the day again and again. Folding girls and now Theo.

She hadn't told Peter about the girl in the library because she wasn't sure it was real. Theo made it more real. She couldn't tell her mother — not yet anyway. She didn't know what she was talking about, and her parents would be scared that not only was Theo losing his mind, but so was she.

The back door banged. Rosemary skidded to a stop. Theo stood on the back porch, slumped against the stone, his eyes on the book in his hands. "Hey, Rosie," he said, his voice flat, stagnant as a pond, but suddenly she felt years younger, and protected.

She slid across the rink and stumbled on the snow. "Hi."

They stared at each other. Or, rather, Rosemary stared at Theo. He stared at his book. The silence stretched between them. Rosemary opened her mouth to say something, but Theo spoke first.

"I — I heard you were in a fight."

Rosemary gaped. "Did Dad tell you?" How did Dad know?

"You shouldn't ... let them get to you," he said, still not looking at her. "They're ... only words."

"Theo, are you all right?"

Theo stood silent a long moment. She could see no change in his expression, but somehow Rosemary sensed that he was considering his answer very carefully.

"Of course I'm all right," he said at last. "Don't worry about me."

"Theo, look at me."

He looked at her. His eyes were glazed and unfocused, as though she were in a fog.

"Theo, I know something's wrong. Is it — is it like high school? Are you sick?"

"No."

She bit her lip. "Is there anything I can do?"

"Rosie, it's okay."

"No, it's not!" Her voice cracked. "I hate to see you like this! I hate —" She halted. "Snap out of it!"

"Rosie, please —" And she was reminded of him in his hospital bed, unresponsive as she tried to reach him.

"It's not fair!" Rosemary shouted. "You're not supposed to be like this! You're the one who protects me, gets me out of fights. You're supposed to be strong!"

His eyes glanced down at the pages as she spoke. He closed them, in pain. "Rosie, please, I'll handle this. I'll be all right. Just … stay away from the books."

She stuttered to a stop. "What?"

"The books." He took a deep breath. "Stay out of this." He turned and stepped back into the house.

"Theo, wait!" She struggled through the snowdrifts after him and scrambled up the back porch. She banged her way into the kitchen and ran into the front room. It was empty. Upstairs, she heard Theo's bedroom door click shut.

As she debated whether to follow, the lights of the station wagon pulled into the driveway. A minute later, her father entered, stomping the snow from his boots. "I drove your boyfriend home, safe and sound, dear!"

"Dad!" She stood with her hands on her hips.

"What?" Her father looked playfully blank.

"He's not my boyfriend!"

"He's your friend, isn't he?"

She faltered. "Well, yes, but —"

"And he's a boy, isn't he? Those are the two criteria for the term, aren't they?"

Rosemary scowled at the floor. "You know what I mean."

Her father nudged her chin. "Yes, dearest. I do."

"How can you be silly at a time like this?"

"It's how I cope."

Rosemary softened. "What do you think happened to Theo?"

Mr. Watson sighed. "I don't know. But we'll find out, dearest. I promise."

Rosemary snuggled beneath the covers, smelling bacon. She could hear the clatter of plates downstairs and the sizzle of the frying pan and she remembered that it was Saturday: pancakes and bacon day. Smiling, she tossed aside the covers and jumped out of bed. She was halfway to the closet when she stopped.

She picked up a grey sweatshirt tossed carelessly over the back of her desk chair. It had a faded group photo on the front of a cast of actors in costume. "Clarksbury High" read the black bold text beneath the photo, and beneath that was a date and "A Midsummer Night's Dream." Theo was in front, dressed as Puck, mugging for the camera. She smiled at his grin, then frowned as she remembered how different he had been last night.

She crept to the door and peered out into the hallway. Theo's door was open and his room was empty. She felt a little hope rise inside her. Was Theo better?

She listened to the voices downstairs. Trisha shouted something across the table. Her father cut her off, calling for quiet and courtesy. Her parents' voices returned to their measured, nervous tones.

Theo's voice didn't come.

Not better.

She sighed and returned to her room. Dressing quickly, she shrugged the sweatshirt on over her clothes and slouched downstairs to breakfast.

Her mother set a plate of pancakes and bacon before Rosemary as she sat down. She cut off a piece with her fork and started chewing. She looked around the breakfast table.

Her mother sat down, poured herself a glass of orange juice, and looked towards the foot of the table. Trisha kicked her chair rails and looked towards the foot of the table. Her father sipped his coffee and looked towards the foot of the table. Theo sat at the foot of the table and read his book.

Her mother's glass of orange juice overflowed, bringing her attention back. Muttering under her breath, she mopped up the spill with her napkin.

The family ate in silence for a moment. Finally, her mother said, "I talked to Doctor Abrams. I'm taking Theo to see him at eleven this morning. It's outside his office hours and he assures me his gossipy receptionist won't be there."

"Why does he keep that kid?" Rosemary's father asked.

"That kid is the only person in this town who can type," her mother replied. "But with him at hockey practice, Theo stands a better chance of privacy. If only that McAllister child hadn't been here to see."

Rosemary bristled. "Peter wouldn't tell!"

"Are you sure?"

Rosemary fought back the flush of anger. It was true that she hardly knew Peter. She should have been as uncertain as her mother.

"Theo had a difficult enough time in high school, thanks to his breakdown." Rosemary's mother ran her hand through Theo's hair. "He doesn't deserve what people will say about this."

"Daddy?" said Trisha. "Is Theo going to be okay?"

He hoisted Trisha onto his knee. "'Course he is. Just as soon as he sees a doctor."

"But Mommy's a doctor," said Trisha.

"Mommy's a doctor of the body," said Mr. Watson. "Dr. Abrams is a doctor of the mind. But don't worry about that. You and I are going out. How would you like to see a movie?"

Trisha smiled. Rosemary could tell that it was for her father's benefit.

In the front room after breakfast, Mr. Watson touched Rosemary's shoulder. "Rose, tell Mrs. McDougall that she's in charge of the library for the day, and help out behind the front desk. Probably won't see another living soul, but hours of operation are hours of operation."

"Sure, Dad," said Rosemary, with a smile that matched Trisha's.

Rosemary refused her father's offer of a lift into town. She pulled her skis from their hooks by the back door and strapped them on. She was on the shoulder of the road before her father and then her mother passed in separate cars. She gave them each a wave and carried on.

The town was a ten-minute trip by ski, much of it downhill. She'd get her exercise coming back, but that was okay. She liked the sound of the skis as they slid over the crusty snow. The bitter wind whistled past her ears. Her cheeks tingled. At the edge of town, she took off her skis and trudged the rest of the way on the sidewalk.

The main library was downtown, one block off of the highway, on the bay side. Mrs. McDougall frowned when Rosemary walked up to the front door and kicked the snow off her boots. "Where's your father?"

"Um, he couldn't come in today." She leaned her skis against the wall. "He told me to tell you you're in charge. I'm supposed to help."

"Hmph. Fine, then. You'll handle the front desk. I'll catalogue the new orders." She bustled off into the back, leaving Rosemary standing by the overnight bin.

The library had few visitors that day. Rosemary set the books aside and twiddled her thumbs at the front desk. She sighed, and frowned to hear it so loud. She was used to the hush of a library, but not to total silence. Perhaps her father should have called it a day off and closed the building; then she thought of Theo. She pulled over an almanac and buried herself in it.

It was early in the afternoon, and Rosemary was pushing the bookcart when she smelled dust again. She stopped, looking up and down the aisle. No one was with her. She was sure that the library was empty, but still she shivered.

The sky outside the front windows was darkening. Another snow squall was coming. She might have to call home to get a lift after all.

Enough was enough. Nobody else was coming. She'd shelve the remaining books and call it a day.

She slid four books into their places on the lower shelves of H–K. The remaining books belonged to the top shelf of L–N. Rosemary looked at the top shelf and sighed. "Growth spurt any day now, Mother says."

Pulling over a stepstool and standing on tiptoe, she was just able to bring her face level with the top-most shelf. She shoved some books aside in order to put a book in their place.

From behind the books, someone stared back at her.

Rosemary gasped.

For a fraction of a second, she thought that she was staring into a mirror and that her reaction had been foolish fright. But another look at those eyes told her that the "reflection" was different.

The girl from the school library was standing on the other side of the bookcase, obviously on her own stepstool. She was glaring at Rosemary, eyes full of resentment and hate. Rosemary was held by those eyes like a butterfly on a pin.

"Who —?"

"Coward!" The girl's voice was as soft as sandpaper. She lashed out, caught Rosemary's wrist, and pulled.

Rosemary screamed. The stepstool flew back as she was pulled into the bookcase. Her forehead hit the top shelf. Another hand grabbed Rosemary's collar. Rosemary kicked, struggled, but felt herself being pulled in.

Then a voice boomed around her. "Hey!"

The grip slackened. Rosemary fell backwards and hit the bookcase behind her. Books rained down on her and the spine of a thick volume clocked her on the head.

Her vision swam. She saw the girl standing over her, sneering. How did she come around the stacks so fast? Rosemary thought she heard someone calling her name, and footsteps running. The girl turned towards the sound and then turned away, folding into herself like paper and disappearing.

When Rosemary's vision cleared, she saw Peter kneeling over her. "Peter!" She grabbed his arm.

"Rosemary! What —"

"There was this girl." She was talking much too fast. "She — she — she was in the — I mean, behind the book-case. She grabbed my wrist. She tried to pull me in —"

"Where did she go?"

"She disappeared."

"Disappeared?!"

"I saw her yesterday, at the school library. She disappeared there too." She stopped suddenly, staring up at Peter in horror. "You don't believe me."

His eyebrows jerked up.

"Of course you don't believe me. Disappearing girls. It's crazy talk, and you know it was just a matter of time."

"What are you talking about?"

"Don't play dumb! You heard the stories about Theo and his breakdown! You have to have heard, everybody knows. Everybody's waiting for me to go crazy too. Of course you don't believe me; *I* don't believe me!"

He looked at her with a gaze that was the most serious she had ever seen. "I believe you."

"But," she sputtered, "why?"

"Because you're bleeding." He nodded at her wrist.

Where the girl had grabbed her, her wrist was covered in thin red cuts, two dozen or more. The cuts made the shape of a hand and clawing fingers. They weren't bleeding much, but they hurt.

"These look like paper cuts," said Peter.

"You believe me." The feeling of relief made Rosemary giggle. "God, Peter, I feel like such an idiot!"

He helped her to her feet. "You're not an idiot."

"But it doesn't help that you believe me," gasped Rosemary. "I mean, it helps, but it doesn't make it go away. If I'm not hallucinating, then something *is* attacking me. Something horrible."

Cold brushed them. The library door had opened.

Peter and Rosemary looked up.

Theo stood in the entranceway.

Rosemary let go of Peter and stumbled over to her brother. He had come in from the cold without a coat. His book was in his hand and he stared blankly ahead.

"Theo?" said Rosemary.

Theo looked at her, then reached out and took her arm, where the girl had cut into her wrist. He stared at the paper cuts, and his gaze grew dark.

"Leave her alone!" he shouted, pointing in Peter's direction.

"What? Theo, no, Peter didn't —" Then Rosemary saw that Theo wasn't pointing at Peter, but at the bookshelves beside him, at the aisle where the girl had been waiting for her.

How did he know?

Theo shouted again, "Leave my sister alone!"

CHAPTER THREE

A WINTER'S TALE

"Please. Why are you doing this?"
— Theo Watson

The library door flew open, and Rosemary's mother burst in, carrying Theo's coat. "Theo!" she cried. "Why did you walk out on us? It's cold! You went six blocks without your coat!" Her breath fogged in the air let in by the door. Theo did not look cold.

"Rosemary needed help." Theo's voice was dull.

"Rosemary's doing just fine, aren't you, dear?" She shot her daughter a look that said, "Just nod!" Rosemary bit her tongue and nodded.

Dr. Abrams came in, puffing. "Theo," he said. "Why did you leave?"

"There is nothing wrong with me," said Theo. "Rosemary needed help."

Dr. Abrams frowned. "That's more responsive than I've seen him all morning."

Rosemary's mother wrung her hands. "Maybe he'd be more comfortable at home?"

Dr. Abrams touched Theo's arm. "Come on, Theo, let's take you home."

Theo shrugged his arm away. "There's nothing wrong with me." There was a rising edge to his voice. "Rosemary needed help."

Rosemary stepped into Theo's vision. "Theo, go with them. Please?"

He focused on her. "Will you be all right?"

She squeezed his hand. "Yes. Peter will help me, won't you, Peter?"

Everybody looked at Peter. He swallowed hard and nodded.

Theo glanced around at the library, blinking at the shelves as though seeing them for the first time. He looked at her. "Watch out for the books. Be home soon."

He turned and walked out the front door. Dr. Abrams followed like a protective dog.

Rosemary's mother gave her a hug. "Thanks, dear. Will you be coming home soon?"

Rosemary nodded. "I'll tell Mrs. McDougall to close up. There's nobody here."

"Hardly anybody downtown, either," said her mother. "But I'm afraid at least a few people saw Theo dashing down the street without his coat. So much for his privacy." She sighed. "I'd wait for you, but —"

"It's okay."

Rosemary's mother followed Theo out of the library.

Rosemary stared through the front window as her mother and Dr. Abrams got Theo into the car and drove off. She sighed, then blinked to feel a hand pat her shoulder. She looked up in time to see Peter hurriedly pull it back.

"What are you doing here?" she said.

He started. "I ... what?"

"What are you doing here?" She turned on him. "I'm here every weekend and I never see you about. Then the day all" — she waved her hands at the stacks where the books lay scattered — "all this happens, you show up. Why?"

He gaped at her. "Why shouldn't I be here? What else is there to do?"

Mrs. McDougall came shuffling out from the back. "Could you two keep that door closed? There's a draft!" She frowned at their stares of disbelief. "What's wrong?"

"Nothing," said Rosemary. "I've just been talking to my mother. Let's close the library early."

"Good idea! I'll get my coat." Mrs. McDougall shuffled to the closet, pulled on her coat, and stepped outside. Peter and Rosemary watched her go.

Peter glanced at her. "Look, I just thought ..."

"I'm sorry." Rosemary took a deep breath. "You've only ever seen me angry or scared. I'm not always like this."

He shrugged and gave her a small smile. "I've seen worse."

She turned to the stacks. "Let's clean up this mess and get out of here."

They put the books back on the shelves, shut down the computers, and turned off the lights. Five minutes later, Peter held Rosemary's skis as she locked the door.

A shape separated from the stacks, a tall figure dressed in green. Through the front windows, it watched Rosemary and Peter walk down the street.

Sunday was also bright and cold. The world was black, blue, and white as Rosemary stepped from the front door of her home. Her breath fogged in the air.

The snow squeaked underfoot as she walked to the mailbox. On days like this, she didn't mind that the newspaper delivery boy didn't bring the paper directly to the front door, even if she had to pull on boots and a coat to get it. She pulled the paper from the mailbox.

A snowball hit her in the back.

Rosemary scowled. *Just call me the snowball magnet*, she thought. She turned around. "Trish, how many times do I have to tell you —"

There was nobody at the front door.

"Ow!" said a voice higher up. Rosemary's gaze shifted to the roof of the house.

A lanky man was perched on the gable above the front door, shaking out a wet hand. "How do you throw these balls of ice?"

Everything about him was odd. His ears were a little too pointed, his arms and legs were a little too long, and his eyes were far too wild. He was dressed like Robin Hood, with a long tunic and hose of green leather.

Oddest of all, he looked familiar.

"Sage Rosemary," he said. "You caught me off my guard. I was asleep, tired from my ordeal. You locked me in the library last night."

Rosemary kept on staring.

"Fortune found me a hatchway to the roof," the man continued. "From there I had no trouble getting down." As if to illustrate, he jumped from the pitched roof, landing nimbly on his feet in front of Rosemary. She kept staring.

He frowned at her silence. "Come, come, Sage Rosemary, surely you do remember me?" He thrust out a long-boned hand. "Robin Goodfellow. You may call me Puck."

Rosemary wheeled around and walked out the front gate and up the country road.

"Rosemary?" Puck called. He followed her.

"Go away!" she shouted over her shoulder.

Two steps behind, Puck matched her pace, his pointy shoes skidding on the snow. "Rosemary, will you not speak with me?"

"You're a figment of my imagination!"

"Do you order all such figments to fly away?"

Rosemary's fists clenched tighter. "A hallucination, then! I'm going crazy at last!"

"Do hallucinations leave footprints?"

She stopped and looked at the road behind Puck. "You don't." She turned again.

Puck looked back at the snow behind him. Only Rosemary's footprints showed. "Oh! How very odd! I wonder why that would be ..." He scratched his chin, and then snapped his fingers. "Of course!" Rosemary was now several paces ahead of him and he bounded after her.

"There is a good reason why I do not leave footprints in your world," he said, matching her pace. "You see, Sage Rosemary, I am not real."

"Is there an echo somewhere?" asked Rosemary.

Puck stopped. "Hallooo!" he shouted. He listened for a moment and then loped after her. "No."

"I already said you weren't real. Now, go away!"

He kept his pace. "Hallucination I am not. They are real after a fashion. Neither am I a sprightly ghost. Figments are as real as a person believes. Wise one, I am not real. I am fiction."

Rosemary stopped. She stared at Puck.

"I am well developed, as you can see." He gave her a smile and twirled around like a ballet dancer. "A three-dimensional character."

Rosemary backed away. She dropped her newspaper. Then she turned and ran.

"Sage Rosemary, come back!" shouted Puck. "I did not mean to frighten you!"

Rosemary ran as fast as her heavy boots would let her, oblivious to her surroundings and any sounds of pursuit. At the McAllister mailbox, Peter was getting his own newspaper. He looked up. "Hey, Rosemary. Where are you go—"

Rosemary ploughed into him. They went down in a scramble of arms, legs, and newsprint.

Peter grabbed her shoulders. "Rosemary!"

She was trembling. "I want my mind back! I want it back, now!"

"Rosemary! What is it?"

She pointed. He looked. The road was empty.

Then, out of nowhere, Puck dropped down in front of them.

Peter and Rosemary yelped.

Wide-eyed, they looked up at the tall, gangly not-exactly-a-man that smiled down at them. The smile might have been meant to be friendly, but Puck's mouth was just too wide, and his eyes just too large and too green.

Rosemary looked sidelong at Peter. "You see him too?"

Eyes wide, Peter nodded.

"Fear not," said Puck.

Peter and Rosemary scampered back.

Puck tapped his foot. "Do you doubt your very own eyes? Shall I prove that I am Robin Goodfellow? Observe my powers, as I transform into a goat!"

And, before their eyes, he changed into a large goat, at least as tall as Puck had been, with green eyes and great curling horns.

Peter and Rosemary clutched at each other and screamed.

The goat rolled its eyes. "Oh, Lord, what fools these mortals be!" He transformed back. "I say again, fear not, for I mean you no harm! Here, let me help you up."

He grabbed them by their wrists, hauled them to their feet, and brushed the snow off them. Peter and Rosemary edged closer together.

"Who is he?" asked Peter. "Where did he come from?"

"He followed me home."

"And you're going to ask your parents if you can keep him?"

Rosemary shoved Peter into the snow bank.

The creature pulled Peter back onto his feet again and shook his hand. "You must be young Peter McAllister, who saved Rosemary at the library," he said. "It is an honour to meet one so valiant. Puck at your service, sir."

Peter's brow furrowed. "Like from *A Midsummer Night's Dream*? That Puck?"

Puck beamed.

"Why are you here?"

"To be Rosemary's guide in her great quest to find her brother, Theo."

Rosemary pushed forward. "You know what's wrong with Theo?"

"He is a prisoner within his mind," said Puck. "You must journey inside to save his hind."

"I must *what*?"

"Come with me to the library," said Puck. "Your quest starts there."

"And if I don't?" demanded Rosemary.

For the first time, Puck stopped smiling. "If you do not, Sage Rosemary, brother Theo will not come back. The hauntings will get worse and worse, alack." He raised a hand as Peter started to speak. "I know your thoughts, young fellow, but be assured that I have naught to do with this. I have no quarrel with Sage Rosemary. I only wish to see her free."

Rosemary and Peter looked at each other. They looked back at Puck. They started to back away.

Puck raised his hands apologetically. "I understand your doubts, my good children. Let me show you that I speak the truth. Go home and go to Theo's room and read the book he's reading. Then you shall understand what ails him." He stepped aside and extended a hand towards the road. They had a clear path.

Rosemary and Peter looked at each other again. Then, giving Puck a wide berth, they ran to the road and back to Rosemary's house.

The house was still asleep. Shamus slunk up the stairs behind them, his toenails clicking. Rosemary led the way to Theo's room.

She pushed open the door. Theo was sitting up in bed, staring into his book.

"Hello, Rosie," he said. He looked up and smiled at her.

He did not look at Peter. His eyes trailed down to his book, and then up again sharply. "Who's your friend?"

"You've met Peter," said Rosemary, shutting the door behind her.

"Really?" said Theo.

"Yes, at the library. And he was over for dinner the day before."

"You brought a boy home for dinner? Good for you." He turned back to his book.

Shamus whimpered. Rosemary patted him. She and Peter crept forward and leaned across the bed to peer at the cover of Theo's book. It was just a normal paperback, with a painted image of a figure in smoke emerging from an open book. But there was no title on the spine.

"It's not a book," she said. "It's a journal; a blank journal!"

Peter peered over Theo's shoulder. "Something's been typed in it." Theo turned the page. The new page started blank, but text appeared in the top left corner and streamed down the paper. "Something's *being* typed into it right now!"

"What?" Rosemary reached for Theo's book.

Theo snapped out of his trance. He pulled the book to his chest. "Rosemary, no!"

She gripped the book by its spine. "Theo, let me see."

Theo shook his head. He wrenched the book back. With a tremendous yank, Rosemary pulled the book out of Theo's grasp.

"No!" Theo's voice choked off.

Rosemary looked at the pages and saw a line saying, "Rosemary looked at the pages and saw a line saying, 'Rosemary looked at the pages and saw a line saying, 'Rosemary looked at the pages and saw a line saying, 'Rosemary looked at the pages and saw —'"

Peter tore the book from her hands.

Rosemary staggered back and covered her eyes.

There was a tapping at the window. Puck's face was centred upside down in the frame, hanging by his feet from the roof. He waved.

Peter opened the window, but Puck did not come in. Instead, he said, "Do you believe me, Rosemary?"

"What the — what happened?" Rosemary gasped, wincing and rubbing her temples.

"I don't know," said Peter. He picked up the book by one corner as though it were something toxic. "You just stared into the pages, and you … froze. You just stood there. I couldn't reach you."

"How long?" asked Rosemary.

"Long enough!" Peter thought a moment. "A minute. You didn't even blink."

Rosemary screwed her eyes tighter. No wonder they hurt.

Peter opened the book.

"Peter, be careful!"

"No, it's okay, I was just reading it. Maybe it doesn't affect me." He flipped to the first blank page. The text was still scrolling down. He frowned.

"It's listing what I've said — what I'm saying right now," he said. He flipped back a few pages. "And here we are talking to Puck in the snow." He grimaced. "Here I am screaming. It's all written from your point of view." He snapped the book closed just as Rosemary was creeping up to peer over his shoulder. "When you looked at the pages as they were being written, you started a loop."

"Theo has been reading the world from your eyes,

Rosemary," said Puck through the window. "Look at your brother now."

Rosemary looked up and then darted forward. "Theo?" She shook her brother by the shoulder. He stared blankly ahead. "Theo!"

"Give him the book," said Puck. "It is his only link to us."

Rosemary pressed the book into Theo's hands. She felt his fingers tighten against the covers. His eyes lowered, and he began to read.

Rosemary held his hands a moment before letting go. "I'm responsible for this?"

"No," said Peter, frowning at Theo. "How could you be?"

Puck shook his head. "You are not the fault, but you are the cause. Because they could not get at you, they stole away your kin."

"What are you talking about?" Peter rounded on the window. "What do you mean, steal Theo? He's right here!"

"No, wait, I see." Rosemary swallowed. "Theo reads more than me. Dad always says he can get lost in a book."

"And now he has," said Puck.

Rosemary turned to the window. "What do I have to do to get Theo back?"

"It won't be easy, Rosemary," said Puck. "You will face dangers only your imagination could dream of."

"I don't *have* an imagination," said Rosemary.

"Of course you do. What else would be attacking you?"

Rosemary stared at Puck, her mouth agape. Then she looked at Theo and drew herself up. "What do I have to do to get Theo back?"

"Come with me to the Land of Fiction," said Puck. "I shall be your guide and Peter your defender, if he be brave enough."

Peter started to say something, but Rosemary cut him off. "First things first, how do we get to this Land of Fiction?"

"We need a book. That is why we must go to the library."

"Why the library?" said Rosemary. "We've got books."

"You do? Even better. Come down and let me in." Puck grabbed the sill and let go of the roof. He twirled in mid-air before disappearing from view. Looking out the window, they saw him on his feet in the snow.

Peter and Rosemary crept downstairs. They jumped when the front door rattled.

Rosemary opened it and found Puck staring at the knocker. It was a carved woodpecker mounted on a pivot; pulling the tail rattled the beak against the wood.

Puck found this fascinating, and Rosemary had to swat his hand away before he pulled the tail again. "You'll wake my parents!"

"Quite." He pulled away from the knocker reluctantly and strode into the living room.

Shamus started at the sight of him. He gave a little growl, but edged forward and sniffed at the hem of Puck's tunic. Then he looked up, let out a quick bark, as he had done when approving of Peter, and stepped away.

Rosemary stared at her dog.

Puck looked at the bookshelves and nodded. "A good collection, Rosemary. Appropriate for one so wise."

"Actually, they're my father's."

"Be that as it may, they are precisely what I need." He pulled a book from the shelves.

Rosemary peered at the cover. "We get to the Land of Fiction through *Jane's World Book of Airplanes?*"

"Any book will do," said Puck. "As long as you can find the secret passage."

"Secret passage?" asked Peter. "What secret passage?"

"Such passages are in all books," said Puck. "You need only to read between the lines." Then, opening the book in the middle, he closed his eyes and began to chant:

A portal opened in the corner of the room,
And filled up with papery light
It gathered until it formed a tunnel
Which stretched onward into infinity.

Then he snapped the book shut and threw it into the corner. The book flopped open on its spine, with its pages fanning out like a fountain. The arches beneath the pages began to glow, and as the glow got brighter, the book grew larger, until the fountain of pages towered over them.

A wind plucked at Peter and Rosemary's clothes, gathering strength until Rosemary was shocked that her parents were sleeping through it. She pushed the hair from her eyes as Puck stepped to the tunnel entrance.

"It will close once you are through, Rosemary," he said. "Pray, do not delay."

He took a step and vanished down the tunnel.

"Right." Peter stepped forward. "Here goes nothing."

Rosemary grabbed his arm. "What are you doing?"

"I'm going with you."

She shook her head. "Theo's already in there because of me. If anything happened to you ..." her voice trailed off. "You're staying right here."

"You can't make me."

"Oh yes I can!"

Still holding Peter's arm, Rosemary used it to try to swing him aside. He struggled. Suddenly they were grappling with each other, each trying to hold the other down and get away so they'd be the first through the portal.

Peter perked up. "Look! It's Theo! He's better!"

Rosemary looked. Peter grabbed her shoulder and shoved her to the floor. He scrambled up and ran, but Rosemary tackled him from behind.

"Got you!"

"So does the portal," gasped Peter.

They were sliding forward on the hardwood floor, the wind blowing them towards the opening, faster and faster. Peter and Rosemary yelled.

The portal closed behind them.

There were shouts from the upper floors as Mr. and Mrs. Watson scrambled out of bed. Theo stumbled downstairs, pawing at the walls like a blind man. He fell into the living room, then picked himself up. Opening the book he glanced around and saw Rosemary's and Peter's unconscious bodies, sprawled together by the corner of the room beside a thick book open on its spine. He was too late.

Shamus sniffed and prodded Rosemary with his snout. She didn't move. He began to howl.

Theo sighed. "Rosemary. Oh, Rosemary, why?" He stood over them, book open, like a priest over a grave.

Rosemary's mother scrambled into the living room. She stopped in the doorway and took in the scene with one glance. "Theo! What did you do?"

Theo closed the book and dropped it on the floor.

Mrs. Watson rounded on her husband, who was steps behind. "Get Trisha out of the house, now. Take her out the back way. Don't let her see this."

Mr. Watson nodded and strode upstairs.

Mrs. Watson stepped into the room, her hair rumpled, her bathrobe askew, looking from her son to her daughter to that McAllister kid. She waved a hand in front of Theo's face and then lowered him into a chair. She took Shamus by the collar and hushed him.

At her feet, Theo's book flipped open with a bang. Mrs. Watson jumped. Then she saw the text streaming down on the page.

Behind her, Mr. Watson bundled Trisha out the back door.

CHAPTER FOUR

THE SEA OF INK

"Revenge, of course. Why else?"
— Marjorie Campbell

Rosemary fell or floated, she could not tell which. Her arms flailed, her hair waved into her eyes, but she felt no wind. When she could see enough to look, she could glimpse only white. She had no sense of up or down.

Then she landed on her back on a surface like a soft mattress. It drove the wind from her lungs and sent up a spray of dust-like fog around her. She lay in a daze and felt the little specks fall back on her.

Slowly, the memories came back: folding girls, Theo, Puck, flying through the paper portal with Peter, then free fall. Now she was here. But where was Peter?

She brushed sand from her cheeks and sat up.

She sat in the middle of a small crater shaped like her outline. The sky was as white as a void, the sand was the colour of snow, and the horizon between them was a thin grey line. The air was still and the temperature felt like it didn't exist. There were no birds. No sound, except for her breath.

She stood up unsteadily, adjusted her glasses, and looked around. She found Peter behind her, spread-eagled and face down in the sand. Rosemary knelt by him and shook his shoulder. "Hey, you okay?"

Peter pushed himself onto his hands and knees and spat sand from his mouth. "I think so."

She helped him to his feet. He rubbed his forehead. "Thanks."

"You're sure you're all right?"

He took a deep breath. "Yeah."

"Good." She slugged him.

He fell over in a spray of dust, then scrambled to his feet. "Hey! Why did you hit me?"

"Because *you* hit *me*!" She rubbed her shoulder.

He blinked at her, then snorted, breaking out into a grin. "Sorry."

Her mouth quirked, but she eyed him sourly. "I told you not to follow me."

He raised his hands. "What did you want me to do? Stand around while you went in alone?"

"I wasn't alone," she snapped. "Puck said —"

"Where is Puck?"

They looked around. They were in the bottom of a bowl of sand so white that, without the sight of each other, they'd have half believed that they'd gone blind.

Their footprints inked the ground like typewriter keys on paper.

"Puck!" Rosemary shouted. Her voice didn't echo.

"Hi ho!" Puck called, his head popping up above the top of a white dune. "Awake, are we?"

"Where are we?" shouted Peter.

"Come up and see." And his head disappeared. They heard a rustling.

Rosemary and Peter glanced at each other and shrugged. They scrambled up the sand dune, stuttering to a stop at the top, blinded by their first sight of black.

Before them stretched a white, sandy beach, ending abruptly at a black sea that slapped at the shore in slow, oily waves. Puck was standing at a grove of gnarled black trees, shaking a branch laden with round white fruit the size of basketballs.

Rosemary and Peter glanced at each other and shrugged again. They trudged to the grove, arriving just as Puck pulled one of the fruits free. "Something to play with while we wait," he said.

"Wait for what?" demanded Rosemary. "Where's my brother?"

"Across the sea." Puck turned Rosemary and Peter by the shoulders and placed his head between theirs. He pointed across the black sea to a speck of colour on the horizon. "There, my friends, look there. That is the Land of Fiction."

"There?" said Rosemary. "How are we going to get over there? You were supposed to bring us *there*! We're going to need a boat."

"We have a boat, wise one," said Puck. "We must wait for the Ferryman."

"The Ferryman?" Peter repeated.

Carrying the white fruit, Puck led the two along the beach. A jetty came into view. No boats were in sight.

Puck sighed. "The Ferryman is never here when one needs him." He flung the white fruit on the ground.

Peter and Rosemary scrambled back, expecting it to splatter. The fruit bounced, changing colour as it hit, swirling like an oil slick on water. The swirls shook as Puck bounced the ball again.

"What is that?" asked Peter.

"An idea — the fruit of an idea tree." Puck grinned.

"Ideas grow on trees?" said Rosemary.

"Where else would they be?" said Puck. "'Tis a shame they are not more common." He bounced the ball once and twirled it to Peter and Rosemary.

Written in black text on a white stripe were the words, "What if rugs could fly?"

Puck bounced the ball again.

The words now said, "What if we could make time run backwards?"

"Ideas fall from the trees and are blown across this beach," said Puck, "and into the great black sea that surrounds the Land of Fiction. In time, they build the Land itself."

Peter reached for the ball. "Let me try!" Puck handed it to him. Peter bounced it.

"What if we could travel at the speed of thought?"

Rosemary stared at the swirling fruit. The words from a book echoed in her mind. She shivered.

"Neat," said Peter. "But why is this 'fruit' made of rubber?"

"So I can do this," said Puck. He snatched up the ball and bounced it off of Peter's head.

He ducked away. "Hey! What are you doing?"

"I am bouncing an idea off you!" Puck held it up. It read: "What am I doing here?"

Peter gaped. "What?"

"Some ideas can be specific to the individual," said Puck. He moved to bounce the ball again.

"Give me that!" Peter grabbed the ball and bounced it off Rosemary's head.

The ball swirled, and a line of text took shape. "What if I can't get Theo back? What if we get stuck here? What if we get hurt? What if we can't —" The line wound around and around until it was like a ball of string.

Puck pulled the ball away. "You are indeed wise, Sage Rosemary. Your mind is full of many thoughts."

Rosemary gaped. "Wait —"

But Puck tossed the ball high into the air. It arced over the beach and landed in the sea. It bobbed on the surface for a few seconds before sinking beneath the waves. "We've had our fun," he said, waving them forward, "but now our ride has come. Move along, my children, along!"

Peter and Rosemary saw movement on the black sea. A boat was gliding across the surface, and a shrouded figure was standing on the prow.

The boat pulled up to the jetty and stopped. The figure floated off. Covered from head to toe in a black cloak, he advanced on the party as though he were gliding on air, though they heard the boards creak beneath him over the slap of oily waves. Peter and Rosemary backed into Puck.

The Ferryman stopped. "Who asks for passage across the Sea?" The voice boomed from the dark space under his hood.

Puck nudged Rosemary forward. She swallowed hard and tried her best to curtsy. Her jeans made it feel silly. "I do."

"And who are you?"

"Rosemary Ella Watson."

"And who are your companions?"

"Robin Goodfellow, her guide," said Puck.

There was a moment's silence, then Puck nudged Peter. He started. "Peter Calvin McAllister."

"The lady's champion," Puck finished.

"What?" squawked Peter.

"And why do you seek to cross?"

Rosemary looked to Puck. He nodded. She turned back to the Ferryman. "To rescue my brother from the Land of Fiction."

"That is worthy," said the Ferryman. "You may now pay the fare."

"The fare?" said Rosemary. "I didn't bring much money —"

"The fare is not money. You must each submit a verse of your own. If I find the three verses good, then all three may cross. If not, another fare is required."

"Oh!" said Puck. "I'll start."

> If we shadows have offended,
> Think but this, and all is mended,
> That you have but slumber'd here
> While these visions did appear.
> And this weak and idle theme,
> No more yielding but a dream,
> Gentles, do not reprehend:
> if you pardon, we will mend:
> And, as I am an honest Puck,
> If we have unearned luck
> Now to 'scape the serpent's tongue,
> We will make amends ere long;

Else the Puck a liar call;

So, good night unto you all.

Give me your hands, if we be friends,

And Robin shall restore amends.

"Hey!" said Peter. "You didn't make that up — William Shakespeare did!"

Puck smiled. "Yes, but those few words first did come from my lips."

The Ferryman bowed. "I accept your verse. Who goes next?"

"I guess I will," said Peter. He took a deep breath.

There once was a bright boy from
    Clarksbury
w-who was confronted with much sound
    and fury ...
He did his best ...
To keep up with the ... rest?
Cause he wanted to go home in a hurry.

The Ferryman considered for a moment, then said, "I accept your verse. And now you, girl."

Rosemary stood, wide-eyed. She opened her mouth, but no words came.

"Rosemary?" said Peter.

She shot him a look of desperation.

Peter stepped towards the Ferryman. "I can do another one."

"No!" The Ferryman pushed Peter back. "It has to come from her."

Rosemary swallowed hard. "One proton, two proton, three proton, four ... hydrogen, helium, lithium ... more?"

The Ferryman looked at her with thundering silence.

Rosemary drooped. Then she looked up. "You said there was another fare?"

"Failing the first fare, instead of three tasks between you, you now have six."

Rosemary went white. "*Six poems?*"

"No. You must show me that you believe in six impossible things before you may cross."

"Like Alice in Wonderland," Peter muttered.

"The White Queen, actually," said Puck. "I'll start. I live within a house the size of a thimble, and I believe that all that I say is a lie."

"Hey!" said Peter. "If everything you say is a lie, then how —"

"Shh," said Puck. "Your turn."

Before Peter could say anything, Rosemary jumped in. "Well, I'm standing right here, and that's impossible."

"Go ahead, take the easy one!" Peter looked as if smoke was going to rise from his head. He turned away and gnawed a knuckle before snapping his fingers.

"Bumblebees!"

"What?" said Rosemary.

"They say it's impossible for bumblebees to fly, but they do!"

"That's because they flap their wings," huffed Rosemary. "If they didn't, they'd drop like stones."

The Ferryman's voice cut between them. "Two more."

They stood in silence, looking around for inspiration. Peter stuffed his hands in his pockets, digging a toe in the paper-coloured sand. The waves slapped the shore. Suddenly he blurted out, "I ... I believe my parents are alive. I wake up and I think that they're downstairs making breakfast and then I ... is that okay?"

"And you?" The Ferryman turned towards Rosemary.

Rosemary had been staring at Peter; she jerked up at the Ferryman's voice. Everyone stood still and silent. Finally a small smile dawned on her face. She took a deep breath. "I believe I can save Theo."

The Ferryman put forth a long hand to the boat. "Board."

They clambered aboard. Peter and Rosemary jammed themselves into a narrow bench while Puck lounged on the remaining seat. The Ferryman stood at the prow. Without oars or sails, the boat glided forward into the sea. As Rosemary glanced at the grey-on-black horizon, Peter nudged her. "Um, the fare … isn't saving Theo the reason we're here?"

She looked at him. "So?"

"So? Well, if you believe it and it's impossible … aren't we in trouble? Or isn't it impossible?"

"Do you want off this boat?" asked Rosemary.

"Just asking!"

Rosemary turned away. She dipped her hand in the water and wrinkled her nose at the faint chemical smell, like permanent markers. "Why is this water so dark?"

"Water it is not, Rosemary," said Puck. "This is the Sea of Ink."

She pulled her arm out. It was black to her elbow. "This is ink?"

"Indelible ink, I fear."

She tried to wipe her arm clean on her jeans, but only smeared them. "Great," she muttered. "Just great."

"The Sea of Ink surrounds the Land of Fiction," said Puck. "It would be wise to keep your hands within the boat. You too, Peter."

He pointed to a wave on the sea. Then Rosemary saw that it wasn't a wave, but the silhouette of a girl, a few years younger than she was, rising out of the water. Her black mouth was open, taking in a great gulp of air before she sank back beneath the waves.

"A character is born," said Puck.

Rosemary shuddered.

Something bumped the boat. Peter and Rosemary looked over the side and saw the dorsal fin of a great black shark sink below the surface. Peter pulled his arm away from the edge. "Can they capsize the boat?"

"No, I think not," said Puck. "The Ferryman has crossed this sea since I was put to paper. Few of his fares have been lost."

"Few?" squeaked Peter.

"The sea is getting thick with characters," said Rosemary.

Other shapes bobbed on the waves. The silhouette of a man in a bowler hat and a suit, carrying a long, black umbrella, walked upright on a swell. He tipped his hat to a teenage girl who cartwheeled past, half submerged. Nearby, a warrior held his black sword high as he sank beneath the surface.

"All the characters in fiction come from here?" asked Rosemary.

"Most," said Puck. "Legendary characters are uncertain of birth, but King Arthur rises every fortnight."

Peter pointed ahead. "I see the other jetty."

The boat coasted up to the jetty and stopped with a crunch against the shore. The beach of white sand stretched ahead for several feet before becoming darker and stonier. Trees rose up further inland, and a forest stretched into the distance.

Puck leapt lightly out and helped Rosemary and Peter step onto the jetty. Then he crossed his arms and bowed low to the Ferryman. He gave Peter and Rosemary a glance, and they mimicked the gesture. The Ferryman bowed in return.

Rosemary started up the beach, with Peter close behind, but Puck stopped them and turned them back to the sea.

"Look," he said. "New characters begin their stories."

Black shapes surfaced from the ink and crawled onto the shore. There, the ink dried on them, changing colour, and they got to their feet as princes and princesses, dwarfs and elves, orphans and detectives, monsters and villains. From the shore, they walked in straight lines to their destinies.

Peter and Rosemary stared after them, awed.

"Come," said Puck, nudging them forward. "Let us begin our own story." And they crossed the beach and slipped in among the trees.

CHAPTER FIVE

INTO THE WOODS

"What did she ever do to you?"
— Theo Watson

Five steps into the trees, Rosemary froze. Peter bumped into her. They looked up and around at the dense canopy and the little slivers of sky. Already they couldn't see the beach that had been behind them. The scenery had changed as completely as if somebody had turned a page.

Puck bounded ahead of them, not bothered by the dense forest. Peter started after, but Rosemary pulled him to a stop. "Wait! Where are we going? What do we do?"

Puck stopped and came back, hunching down to Rosemary's height, his hands on his knees. "The Land of Fiction is a patchwork of stories," he said, "each with its own setting and its own challenge to face. We proceed through them until we find and rescue Theo."

"But where is Theo?" asked Rosemary.

"That's easy," said Peter. "If he's a prisoner in a storybook, then he is in a dungeon, right? How many dungeons are there in the Land of Fiction?"

"Four hundred and sixty-two thousand, five hundred and ninety-three," said Puck.

Peter's face fell.

"But we will not find Theo in a dungeon," said Puck. "Find one and you will find them all; it is too insecure. No, to find Theo, we must proceed to the centre of the island." He waved them forward.

Rosemary didn't move. "Why the centre of the island?"

"Because it is the highest point of land," said Puck. "It is a goal to strive for. Once we reach the peak, we will come to the climax of our story, and you will find Theo."

"That's kind of stupid," said Peter.

"Tsk, tsk! Trust your native guide!" Puck beckoned Peter and Rosemary forward.

Peter and Rosemary glanced at each other, and then stopped in their tracks. They stared at each other, then at themselves.

Their clothes had changed. Instead of jeans and a winter coat, Peter was wearing a medieval tunic and stockings, leather shoes, and a leather cap with a feather sticking out of it. Slung over his shoulder was a longbow.

Rosemary was in a pink and white dress that stretched to her ankles. There was something on her head. She tried to yank it off. "Ow!"

After pulling off the pins, she disentangled a cone-shaped storybook princess hat. "I look like a fairy godmother! A *short* fairy godmother!"

Puck sighed and stepped back.

"Why did our clothes change?" asked Peter.

"To make you more suitable to the setting," said Puck.

Rosemary cast aside her cone hat. She poked her foot out from beneath the hem of her dress and peered at her cloth slippers. "How am I going to get through the forest in this?"

"How come —" Peter's eyes went wide. "Oh, no — we're part of a story, aren't we?"

Rosemary looked up. "Peter?"

He shivered. "Think about it: a storybook forest? Bad things happen in storybook forests! We could run into lions or tigers or bears —"

"Lions live in grasslands," said Rosemary.

"I'm talking *storybook* forests!" Peter rounded on Puck. "What's here? Goblins? Trolls? Evil trees?"

Puck shrugged. "That, my friend, I cannot say. We must go on and find the way." He linked their hands together. Peter and Rosemary looked at each other and let go. They grabbed hold again when

Puck took Rosemary's other hand and pulled her into the forest.

Puck soon let go of their hands and darted ahead of them, prancing and leaping over fallen logs, looping back to them to make sure they weren't left behind.

"I had a dog like this," muttered Peter, his arms folded and his shoulders hunched. "Maybe we could throw him a stick."

"I don't see why you're so worried," said Rosemary. "Look at Puck. He seems at home here."

Puck turned around and paced them, walking backwards. "That is because this *is* my home!" He swung his arms wide. "And I am always happy to return to it! I am the forest and the forest is me. Remove me and a part is lost. Return me and I am whole!"

He cartwheeled backwards, landing on his feet. "Dance with me, Rosemary!" He held out his hand. "Feel the joy of the forest!"

Rosemary hung back, but Puck caught her hand. She sailed into the dance with a cry. Then, as Puck swung her around, she began to laugh and shriek with delight.

Puck twirled her, and Rosemary, laughing, swung down the path towards Peter. She reached out her hand to draw him into the dance, but he ducked back. She stopped and looked at him sourly. "Why not?"

He laughed. "I — I'm not the dancing type."

"You should be," said Puck. "You seem most nimble and well-made. Doesn't he, Rosemary?"

"I — I just think we should be more careful," stammered Peter.

"How can you be afraid of this place?" said Rosemary. "With Puck so happy, what could possibly go wr—"

Puck tackled her, clamping a hand over her mouth. Rosemary struggled free. "What?"

"You tempted fate," said Puck, his smile gone. "Never do that in the Land of Fiction."

"But this is your home!"

"Sage Rosemary, look me in the eye. I am the forest and the forest is me. Would you trust *me* every moment of the day and night?"

Rosemary looked at Puck. His eyes were bright as new leaves and deep as wells. They sparkled with energy and Rosemary was bathed in Puck's compassion for her. But she also sensed a wildness in that gaze that could overwhelm her.

She turned away, shivering. "I'm sorry. I wasn't thinking!"

"My fault. You caught my happiness. You could not see my caution."

Peter cut them off. "I hear something."

A low and steady drumbeat rose at the edge of hearing and grew louder.

Peter, Puck, and Rosemary dove for cover in the bushes. From there they watched the path and listened.

The drumbeat grew louder, and as it did, other music, whistles and trumpets, entered the range of hearing. Then they heard the sounds of marching feet, and they could see shapes moving along the path.

As the figures came closer, Peter and Rosemary realized that the shapes weren't human, they were ... shapes. And they were singing.

> Two, four, six, eight,
> Find the greatest numerate!
> Three, six, nine, twelve,
> Through the forest we will delve!
> Four, eight, twelve, sixteen
> To catch the largest number seen!
> Five, ten, fifteen, twenty
> For our hunt to feed us plenty!

Spheres, cubes, and pyramids, each barely two feet tall, were marching along the forest floor on legs as thin as pencils. Their hands were human, but barely an inch across. Their arms were as thin as their legs. They wore white sailor hats, white gloves, and galoshes and carried fountain pens for spears.

Rosemary frowned. She stood up.

"Rosemary!" Peter gasped. "What are you doing?"

She stepped through the bushes and onto the path. Peter moved to stop her, but Puck held him back. "She is following her instinct. My instinct says to let her."

The troop of shapes stopped in their tracks. They looked at Rosemary in shock.

One of the shapes, a gold sphere with two white eyes, a slit mouth, and no nose, stepped forward. It peered at Rosemary. "Princess Rosemary!" it squealed in a little-girl voice. It jumped up and down. "You're back! You're back! It's been one-two-three-four-five-six-seven-*eight* years since you last read us!" The creature jumped into Rosemary's arms and looked her over. "You've grown!"

Rosemary lifted the little sphere in shocked delight. "Una? I remember you!" She looked around at the crowd. "I remember all of you! You're the Number Crunchers!"

A cheer went up among the crowd. "She remembers us! She remembers us!"

"I read you when I was like four!"

"And eight years have passed," said Una. "That makes you twelve, because four plus eight is twelve!"

"Yes, I know that." Rosemary hesitated, blushing. "I can divide and multiply."

"Ooo!" said the crowd.

Peter and Puck glanced at each other, shrugged, and stepped out of the bushes.

The Number Crunchers gasped and started to edge away.

"It's okay," said Rosemary. "These are my friends." She looked at Peter. "Why are you snickering?"

"So, this was what you were reading when you were four?" said Peter.

Another shape darted forward, two blue pyramids balanced tip to tip. It hopped into Peter's arms. "Peter the Valiant of the Merry Men! It's been one-two-three-four-five-*six* years since you last read us!"

Peter flushed. "Hello, Dué."

The crowd cheered. "Not just one reader returns, but two! Hurray! What a joyous reunion for the Number Crunchers! A feast! We must have a feast to celebrate!"

The shapes scrambled and produced a blanket from nowhere. They spread it out along the path and began setting down plates, forks, knives, and cups. Then came the platters of food.

Peter leaned towards Rosemary. "What are they serving us?"

She grinned at him. "Numbers, of course! Why else would they be called the Number Crunchers?"

"Can we eat numbers?" asked Peter.

"Certainly," said Dué, pulling something from her backpack. "Here, have a four."

Other numbers were being laid out on large platters, garnished with operands. Other shapes were mixing various drinks together to the precise millilitre. Number Crunchers ushered Peter, Rosemary, and Puck forward to the guest of honour positions. Rosemary placed Una beside her and sat down. Puck sat cross-legged, all points: elbows, knees, and chin. The others followed, until the blanket was ringed with geometric shapes, two humans, and Robin Goodfellow.

Peter took his four and sniffed it. He chewed at the stem and swallowed. "This tastes like beef jerky."

"They do say math is dry," said Puck.

Rosemary broke a four in half. The pieces reshaped themselves in her hands into smaller twos. She took a bite out of one and picked up a glass. "Try the numerade."

Una was staring at Puck. "You know Robin Goodfellow?" she said to Rosemary. "You have moved up in your reading, Princess Rosemary. Has he been treating you well? Not leading you down mischievous paths, I hope. You are still quite young."

"He's fine." Rosemary frowned. "He's my guide through the Land of Fiction."

"Why *are* you trekking through the Land of Fiction, Princess Rosemary?"

"To rescue my brother."

A hush fell over the crowd. Rosemary caught whispers: "Theo! We remember Theo! He read us fourteen years ago. She took him. Rosemary is going up against Her. Oh, poor Princess Rosemary!"

Rosemary frowned. "You know about this?"

Una nodded sadly. "We have heard rumours."

"Who's kidnapped my brother? You said 'her.' Do you mean a girl, like me, wearing horn-rimmed glasses?"

"We don't know for sure," said Dué. "She is hard to read. All we know is that she is a powerful character. We stay out of Her way. Don't go to Her, Rosemary. We don't want you to be hurt."

"She has no choice," said Una. "She has to save her brother."

"What does she want?" asked Rosemary. "Why did she kidnap Theo?"

"Because She is very angry," said Una.

The other numbers nodded and repeated, "Very angry. Very, very angry."

Una continued. "She is angry at you."

Rosemary gaped at her. "Me? What did I do?"

"We don't know," said Dué. "We do not understand Her. We know you, Rosemary. You have been nothing but good to us."

"Great to us!" clamoured the crowd. "We had such fun!"

"We learned how to add together," said Una.

"And subtract," said Dué.

"We made the numbers dance," said Una. "Do you remember how we danced?"

Peter sunk his head into his hands. "Oh God, I remember. There was dancing."

"Wait a minute," said Rosemary. "What about —"

A clatter of musical instruments interrupted her. A group of shapes holding fiddles, banjos, a washing board, and a milk jug scrambled together and started a tune. Other shapes took partners while a purple dodecahedron strode out to call the cues.

"Now bow to your partner. Now bow to the corner."

"They're square dancing," said Peter.

Una began pulling on Rosemary's fingers, her galoshes squeaking. "Come! Dance with us, Princess Rosemary!"

"But," said Rosemary. "Hey!"

Dué pushed at Peter from behind. "You too, Peter!"

"But," Peter stammered. "I — I'm not the dancing type!"

"Me neither," said Rosemary, gripping the ground with her free hand. "I — I couldn't. Puck? A little help, here!"

"Certainly," said Puck, and pushed them onto the dance area.

Peter and Rosemary stood up, facing each other. Rosemary swallowed hard. Dué and Una joined hands as the cue caller spoke up. "Now swing your partner round and round ..."

Rosemary and Peter tried reaching for each other's hand, got mixed up, and ended up slapping wrists twice. Una and Dué darted between their legs to opposite corners, and Peter and Rosemary had to shove past each other to complete the square.

"Crossproduct allemande!" called the cue caller.

"Crossproduct what?" said Peter.

"Like this," whispered Una, twirling Dué between them. Peter and Rosemary hesitated a moment, then stepped into the square. This time Peter took Rosemary's hand and she twirled, planting her foot directly on his toe. He stumbled, bumped her. She staggered. "Sorry!" They scrambled for their corners.

"Corner cross times two!" called the caller.

Rosemary switched places with Una through the centre of the square. Peter crossed with Dué. That had gone much better.

"Now do-si-do the cosine wave through all four corners of the square!"

Rosemary and Peter followed Una and Dué's movements and managed to pass each other without stumbling. As they passed again, Rosemary flashed Peter a triumphant grin.

"And with your partner, promenade! Promenade! Promenade!"

Arm in arm, Peter and Rosemary strode down the path; Una and Dué marched behind them.

At once, the music stopped, and Peter and Rosemary stood on their own, arm in arm, on the forest pathway. The Number Crunchers were nowhere to be seen. They glanced at each other, then stumbled apart, taking a keen interest in the surrounding foliage.

The sound of Puck applauding brought their attention around. They looked up to see him leaning against a tree. "Congratulations, my friends. You have passed the first challenge."

"What are you talking about?" said Rosemary. "Where did Una go?"

"She sends her best wishes," said Puck, hauling out a leather-bound pouch. "And numerous leftovers from your feast. As for what I speak about, you passed the first challenge; you danced it all away."

"That's the challenge?" said Peter. "Where's the challenge in that?"

"Did it come easy to you?" said Puck.

Peter frowned. Then the light dawned. "Oh."

"I wish we'd got a chance to say goodbye," said Rosemary. "They were just as fun as I remembered."

Peter snorted. "And you said you had no imagination."

"I was four!" said Rosemary. "Everyone has an imagination when they're four!"

"And no one loses it," said Puck. "If they show it not later in life, they have merely locked it away. And such tyranny can lead to rebellion."

Silence fell on the forest. Puck eyed Rosemary, his arms across his chest. Peter glanced from one to the other, looking perplexed. Rosemary lowered her gaze to the ground.

She clenched her fist. "Come on. Let's find Theo."

She strode forward, Peter and Puck following, deeper into the woods.

CHAPTER SIX

A DARK AND STORMY NIGHT

"Nothing. That's the point!"
— Marjorie Campbell

They'd walked for an hour when suddenly Rosemary's shoes changed. She stumbled and fell over.

She sat up, dusting herself off while Puck came back and watched with amusement. She was wearing a dress of heavy brocade with billowy skirts and frills around her neckline. No pink princess dress, this. She slapped away Puck's helping hand and struggled to get up. Then she gave up and clasped his wrist, hauling herself to her feet. She glared at his cheeky grin. "New clothes. New story?" she asked. Puck nodded. "What's it about?"

"I think I know," came Peter's muffled voice. Rosemary turned. Her eyes widened, then she clamped a hand over her laugh.

Peter clanked up to her in a full suit of armour. Only a narrow slit allowed him to see. "No fair!" he said, pointing at her with jointed gloves. "Why can't *you* be the knight in shining armour?" He slid up his visor. "It's not funny! I can't breathe in this —" His next words were cut off as the visor clanked down.

Then Rosemary's gaze fell on Peter's scabbard, and she stopped laughing. She eyed the jewelled hilt of the sword it contained, and the length that trailed behind Peter. She glanced once more at her own dress, ludicrous, but more realistic. "Puck? Where are we?"

He shrugged. "That I cannot say. Read on, go on, my friends. The answer awaits us!" He bounded off. Peter and Rosemary glanced at each other. Peter shrugged with a clatter. They followed.

They soon heard the sound of running water, and as they rounded a curve in the path they came upon a narrow stone bridge rising above a swift forest stream. Its threshold was guarded by two chrome jaguars.

Rosemary halted by the jaguars. "What the ..."

"What?" Peter thrust up his visor and peered. "What are these oversize hood ornaments doing here?"

Puck was staring at the air over the bridge, rubbing it with his finger. He looked at the two. "What troubles you?"

"These," said Rosemary, tapping the metal snouts with her finger. "Princess outfit, suit of armour, stone bridge, and metal panthers or whatever? Did we step into a 'what's wrong with this picture' book?"

Puck peered around as though looking for cameras. Rosemary threw up her hands. "Let me guess: 'That I cannot say'!"

He grinned at her. "No. That I do not know." He pointed a long finger over the stream. "What I do know is that the challenge lies before us. To leave this story, we must go across the bridge and continue on our way."

"That's it?" said Peter. "Where's the challenge in that?"

On the other bank, a knight in black armour stepped out from behind a tree and clanged his way onto the bridge. He had a sword with a pommel as large as a skull.

"Me and my big mouth," said Peter.

The Black Knight drew his sword. "Did I hear somebody utter a challenge?" he bellowed. He pointed his sword at Peter. "Is the boy fool enough to challenge me to a duel to the death?"

Peter's eyes went round, then the visor clanked in place in front of them. He struggled with his scabbard and drew his sword. The weight of it almost made him drop it.

Rosemary gulped. "This isn't fair!" she said to Puck. "How can Peter fight *him*?"

"It is a quest, Sage Rosemary. It is not meant to be fair."

"But —"

The Black Knight raised his sword and charged with a mighty yell. Puck and Rosemary ducked out of his way. Sword and helmet flying, Peter ran into the woods. The knight thundered after him.

"Puck, do something!" Rosemary shook him. "He can't fight that knight alone!"

Puck shook his head sadly. "I cannot."

Peter dashed out of the forest, tearing off his gloves and clawing at his breastplate, the Black Knight at his heels. "Turn, boy! Face me!"

"Puck!" shouted Rosemary. "Help him!"

"I am but a guide, Sage Rosemary," said Puck. "It is your quest, and so it is your challenge."

"Peter's challenge," said Rosemary. "The Black Knight is going after *him*!"

"And your challenge too," said Puck, tapping her forehead with a long finger. "*You* must save Peter."

"But how can I? I don't even have a sword!"

"Remember, Rosemary, a hero has a thousand tricks."

Rosemary turned towards the sound of the Black Knight's voice.

Peter dashed back into view, the Black Knight even closer behind him. "When I catch you, you quick cur, the pieces of you will fly faster than your legs now carry you!"

Peter ran past Rosemary, not seeing her in his panic, and disappeared into the trees again. Rosemary took a deep breath and stuck her foot into the path of the Black Knight.

He tripped and went down. There was a clatter like someone dropping a whole kitchen full of dishes.

Rosemary rubbed her ankle. "Will that do?" she asked. Puck nodded.

The Black Knight was sprawled face down on the muddy path, embedded inches into the earth, trapped by the weight of his own armour. His sword stuck out of the ground, well beyond his reach. Rosemary yanked it up and then staggered to hold it.

Peter slunk out of the forest. "Some champion I turned out to be," he muttered. Rosemary patted his shoulder. Puck smoothed out his dishevelled hair.

"My lady!" came the muffled voice of the Black Knight. "You do not fight fair! You should not fight at all!"

"I'm not a lady. Get up!"

"Help me."

Rosemary shook her head. "I don't trust you."

"I am a man of honour," said the knight. "I will not take advantage. Please, my lady, the mud is blocking my visor — I cannot breathe!"

Rosemary started to say something, but Peter raised a hand. "Do you yield?" he said to the knight.

"It was not a fair fight!"

"Peter's twelve and you're claiming you lost unfairly?" said Rosemary.

"Never mind that," said Peter. "Do you yield, or shall we leave you where you lie?"

"I yield!" shouted the knight. "Just turn me on my back!"

Straining, Rosemary and Peter managed to roll him over. They watched as the knight pulled off his helmet and lay back, gasping. He had a weathered face and a dark, scruffy beard. He looked hard at Rosemary, and his eyes widened. "The Lady Rosemary!" he exclaimed. "So, you have returned after all this time!"

Rosemary jerked back. "Returned?"

"Has it not been six years since you saw me carry off the beautiful princess to the Castle of Doom?" said the knight.

"I saw —" Her brow furrowed. "Wait, I remember! You stole her from the church where she was going to be married. What happened to her?"

"She is still in the Castle of Doom, across the river."

Rosemary hoisted the sword's tip level with the knight's nose. "What have you done with her?"

"Why, nothing, my lady. You left the story at that point. It does not go forward without you."

"It will now," Rosemary snapped. "You're going to let her go!"

"My lady, I —" the Black Knight began.

"We beat you, right?" said Rosemary. "You have to do what we say, right? So, I say you let the princess go, right now!"

The Black Knight sagged. He picked himself off the ground and limped between the chrome jaguars and over the bridge. "This way, Lady Rosemary."

As Rosemary followed, Peter touched her shoulder. "You okay?"

She shivered. "She just screamed. Screamed all through the forest, and nobody came to save her."

"She didn't get away?" asked Peter.

"I don't know. I — I didn't read any further."

Puck gave her shoulder a squeeze. He took the sword from her and swung it up to his shoulder like a swagger stick.

They crossed the bridge and followed the pathway until they came to a clearing in the forest. At the centre of the clearing stood a tall, round tower of stone, barely ten feet across, its peak poking above the forest canopy. Windows rose up the sides, and a heavy oak door blocked the entrance.

The Black Knight stepped to the door and knocked. "Princess Asphodel!" he shouted. "I have been defeated in" — he hesitated, then continued in a grumble — "fair combat. I release you. Come down and meet your rescuers."

A sound like a snake's hiss started up from somewhere above them. Rosemary's eyes tracked up to the second-storey window and she stepped back.

Framed in the window was a tall princess with long golden hair, wearing a pale green dress. The hissing was coming from her lips, which were drawn back from a toothy snarl.

The hiss became a yell, and the princess leapt from the window, coming down with all of her ninety-eight pounds on Rosemary, knocking her to the ground.

Peter rushed forward, but the princess knocked him aside with the back of her hand. Puck lunged, but the princess punched him in the stomach and chopped him in the back of the neck. Then she rounded on Rosemary.

"Six years!" Princess Asphodel screamed. "Six years I waited for rescue! Six years cooped up in that hideous tower with no decent bath, barely a decent larder, and only that smelly lout for company!" She jabbed a finger at the Black Knight. "If you ever *once* thought of washing yourself, I might have settled for you, but no!"

She pushed Rosemary down. "Do you think you can rescue me after six years and expect me to be grateful? Do you?"

The Black Knight rushed forward. "Princess," he pleaded, placing a hand on her shoulder. "Please, calm yourself —"

The princess jumped up, grabbed the Black Knight by the arm, and swung him into the castle wall. There was a great clang of metal against stone. "Calm myself?" she screamed. "You kidnap me and leave me to rot, and you tell me to calm myself!"

She swung the knight around again, smashing him back into the castle wall. His helmet clattered on the ground. She snatched it up, jumped onto the Black Knight's shoulders, and jammed the helmet down, backwards, over his head. He flailed about blindly. Then she jumped down, picked up the sword that had fallen from Puck's grip, and smacked the flat against the side of his helmet. He yelled and clutched at his ears.

She hit him again with the flat of the sword, this time against the back of his head. She followed up with a kick to the back of his knee and a hard push against his shoulders. The Black Knight toppled face down in the mud. He lay still.

The princess dropped the sword, spat on the knight, and spat on Rosemary. Then she drew herself up, straightened her hair, took a deep breath, and ran, wailing, across the bridge and into the forest.

Peter gaped after her. "She didn't seem too happy to be rescued."

Puck was already standing, brushing himself off. "She did wait six years. How would you feel after such time?"

Rosemary sat up, breathing heavily. "Why couldn't she have rescued herself?"

"It was not in her character," said Puck.

As Rosemary and Peter rolled the dazed knight onto his back, Rosemary asked, "How many more challenges do we face before we find Theo?"

Puck shrugged. "It depends on the length of our tale. Sometimes we face three challenges, sometimes as many as seven."

"Seven?" Peter exclaimed in horror. "Why?

"It is the law."

"The law?" echoed Peter.

"Certainly," said Puck. "In every story there must be a hero." He nodded at Rosemary. "And in every story there must be a damsel in distr..." He trailed off. He was pointing at Peter. Peter folded his arms.

Then they heard something on the bridge that made them turn around.

Sniffing at the base of the bridge were the two chrome jaguars, their roughed-in eyes staring blindly. Their noses snuffed the pathway.

Rosemary tensed. What scent could they be looking for, but hers and Peter's?

The jaguars stopped sniffing. Their heads came up towards Rosemary and Peter. They growled, their bared teeth reflecting the light.

"I told you those things weren't natural," said Peter.

Puck pulled the helmet off the Black Knight. "Sir Knight, see those metal animals yonder? How came they to be here?"

The Black Knight staggered to his feet. "I do not know. I have never seen them before."

The jaguars crouched low and took slow, measured steps towards the party.

The knight picked up his fallen sword. "Lady Rosemary, get your friends down the pathway. That is the way to the next challenge. I shall fend these creatures off."

"They're made of metal," said Peter. "You wouldn't stand a chance!"

"Do not argue!" shouted the knight. "These creatures are not part of your challenge. Go!"

The jaguars snarled and charged.

Puck grabbed Peter and Rosemary's wrists and they ran down the path. Behind them, the jaguars roared, and they heard the screech of metal against metal.

Chapter Seven

A TIGHT SQUEEZE

"I don't understand."
— Theo Watson

They ran. Peter stumbled in the bits of armour he couldn't get off. Puck led them along a streambed to cover their scent, and then along the forest path until Peter begged for rest. Puck left them gasping, and listened to the forest for signs of pursuit.

"I hear nothing," he said when he came back. "We have left our pursuers far behind."

Rosemary wiped her face on her brocade sleeves. Her long skirts were soaked and torn.

"What were those things?" panted Peter. "I never read about things like that."

Rosemary hefted her skirts and marched ahead. "Come on. Let's get out of here."

They followed the forest path until it suddenly spilled onto a large, well-tended lawn, rolled into hills and dotted with pruned hedges. Roiling clouds covered the sky. The wind picked up.

Rosemary paused, took a deep breath, and stepped out onto the smooth green grass.

She doubled over. "Ack!" She clutched her stomach. "What am I wearing?" She struggled to take a breath.

Blue and green taffeta covered her from neck to toe. Instead of her glasses, gilt pince-nez pinched her nose, attached to a ribbon around her neck. The dress had a bustle, and the waist was alarmingly tight.

"I — I think it's a Victorian dress," said Peter. He was wearing flannel pants, a starched shirt, an ascot tie, and an evening jacket.

"What's it made of?" Rosemary gasped. "I feel like I'm being squeezed to death by a picket fence. I've got to get this off!"

"What?" Peter stumbled back.

"Wait here." She staggered away from Peter and Puck and slipped behind the cover of a hedge. Immediately, the bushes began to quake and rustle as she gruntled and yelled. The dress flew into view, followed by a mound of crinolines, which blew away like white tumbleweeds. Still the grunting and snapping of branches continued.

Peter shivered in the freshening wind. "What's taking her so long?" He looked up at Puck, who just raised an eyebrow.

Rosemary let out a sound like a large animal straining against its leash. Then she stopped. The quaking bushes stopped. For a moment there was silence. And then Rosemary rasped, "Help!"

Peter and Puck bolted for the bushes. Peter grabbed a branch to pull himself around the corner, then stopped dead. Puck nimbly dodged him and stood, tense as a gazelle.

Rosemary was on her knees, gasping for air. She was dressed all in white, bloomers and camisole still covering her. From the waist up, she was clamped inside a vicious whalebone corset. She looked up at them, eyes wide. "I can't ... I can't get this ... off! I can't ... breathe!"

Puck let out his breath. A smile touched his lips. "Easy, now, Sage Rosemary." He touched the top of her head. Her rapid breathing eased, though she still couldn't take a full breath.

"I'm ... I'm sorry," she gasped. "I feel stupid. The knot won't come loose." She turned her back to him, revealing a line of woven string more intricate than a suspension bridge.

"There, there," said Puck. "There is no knot I have not beaten." He touched the ropes gently and they parted. He tugged the corset apart.

Rosemary took a deep, rasping breath. She pulled the corset over her head and sent it flying with a kick. She stood, breathing heavily, in camisole and bloomers. She looked up at Puck. "Thanks."

Peter gaped at the corset. "Women wore those things?"

She grinned. "Not anymore." She picked up her fallen overdress with her ink-stained arm and cleared her throat.

Peter turned beet red and darted around the bushes. Puck stared after him quizzically, then shrugged and followed.

As the wind picked up, Peter and Puck stood waiting at the edge of the grounds as the bush rustled, then Rosemary emerged, clad in her overdress, hem trailing on the ground.

"Are you all right, Sage Rosemary?" asked Puck.

She rubbed her side. "My stomach hurts, but it could be from Princess Petunia jumping on me."

"Asphodel," said Puck.

"Whatever." She finally noticed her new glasses and snatched them off to peer at them.

"Um, Rosemary?" Peter gestured. "Y-you missed some of the buttons." Her dress gapped at the back of her waist.

Rosemary gave Peter a look. He raised his hands. "Never mind."

"We make progress with every step," said Puck, "so let us not stop here. Come!" He led the way across the grounds.

Rosemary's dress was too long now that it wasn't held out by crinolines. She stumbled over the hem several times, and finally, nearing the crest of a hill, she tripped on it and fell over. "This is ridiculous! The sooner we finish this challenge the better!" Peter helped her up. "What do we have to do?"

Puck was standing up the slope, looking over the hill. "Keep our feet, Sage Rosemary. And keep our heads."

Peter loosened his ascot and handed it to her. "Here. Belt it up."

Rosemary hoisted her skirts and tied the grey sash around her waist. Thunder rolled across the sky. "I hope this challenge is indoors. Puck, what are you looking at?" She came up to the crest of the hill and stopped in her tracks. "Oh, no."

A mansion of dark stone and crooked shutters frowned across at them. Behind it, a towering black cloud flashed with lighting. At the roof's peak, a weathervane in the shape of a running maiden spun wildly. They could hear its little metal cries.

Rosemary took a step back, pressing into Puck. "I know what this is," she said. "I know enough to know we shouldn't go in there!"

"But the challenge —" Puck began.

"I don't care about the challenge!" said Rosemary, shaking. "We go around or something."

Peter was ahead of them by a few paces, standing just past the crest. "Or something?" he echoed. "Rosemary, look at this."

Rosemary and Puck climbed the rest of the way to him and looked.

The front door of the house was before them. The wings of it stretched out on either side, and kept on stretching. Rosemary's gaze followed the roofline as it rolled over the hills to the darkening horizon, like the Great Wall of China. "That's not fair!"

Puck squeezed her shoulder. "It is the Land of Fiction. It is not meant to be fair."

Lightning flashed. Peter blinked. "Look, a Zeppelin! Isn't it bad for them to be out in storms?"

Rosemary started and followed Peter's pointing finger. In the distance, a long, cigar-shaped airship hovered over a wing of the house. She looked down at her dress and back towards it. "Did they even *have* Zeppelins back ... uh ... now?"

Peter shrugged.

Puck stepped forward, rubbing his chin. "A ship that floats in the sky? My, my!"

The airship made a slow turn towards them. Rosemary shivered. Lightning flashed again. "Come on. Let's get inside before it rains." She led the way down the hill to the front door.

Peter and Puck followed as she crunched across the gravel driveway. A single crow cawed, and there was a rumble of thunder. Rosemary craned her neck up at the grey face of the house and hesitated. Peter eased her forward, up the marble steps.

Thunder cracked. Rain started suddenly, coming down in torrents. As Rosemary reached up to knock, the door creaked opened by itself.

"Oh, that can't be good," said Peter.

"Nope," said Rosemary. Without thinking, she took his hand. Together, they stepped inside.

They entered a panelled lobby, hung with huge portraits and rusting swords. Dim gas lamps filled the space with flickering shadow. Heavy velvet drapes stirred in cold drafts. They edged forward, footsteps echoing. The door creaked closed behind them and shut with a click. Peter shivered. "What do we do now?"

Rosemary shrugged. "Get through the house, I guess. We look for a back door. I just hope nobody notices us." They stepped forward.

Rosemary felt something tug at her hem and she whirled around. A suit of armour staggered forward and she ducked back with a scream. The armour toppled to the floor, smashing to pieces with a gigantic crash. The metal clatter echoed and re-echoed through the house for several minutes before finally dying down.

Peter bit his lip. Puck avoided her eyes. Rosemary stood surrounded by pieces of armour, the hem of her dress still snagged on the axe handle. She yanked it free. "I hate this dress," she muttered.

"Think somebody noticed us?" said Peter.

"Shut up!"

The wind rose. It snuffled into small holes and openings and moaned down the hallways.

Peter and Rosemary drew closer together. "I have a bad feeling about this," he said.

"Yeah. Come on."

They started forward. Then a trap door opened beneath their feet and they fell with a single scream.

Peter and Rosemary found themselves sliding down a chute. They smashed through a swinging door and then they were rolling across a carpeted hallway, landing in a tangled heap against a wall. Puck somersaulted out of the hatch and landed nimbly on his feet beside them.

Rosemary's skirts had flown up and tangled around her head. She felt as if she were tied in a sack. She flailed her way free. "Right!" she said. "That's *it*! I might have to do a haunted house, but I won't do this stupid dress!" She tore at it, sending tiny black buttons flying. She yanked the skirt back up over her head.

"Rosemary, w-what are you doing?" Peter stuttered. White undergarments were emerging from the tangle of blue and green. "Calm down!"

"I'll be ... calm," she grunted, struggling inside the taffeta. "I'll be ... calm ... as soon ... as I get ... this thing ... off!" Rosemary's head burst out of the dress, and she flung it aside in triumph. Her Victorian updo was a frizzled wreck. "There," she said. "Now I'm calm!"

She stood up and saw Peter staring at her bloomers and camisole, agog. "What?" she said. "I'm wearing lots!"

"Well, yeah, but all of that's underw—" He faltered. "I mean, you're —" Silence stretched. "You look fine." He turned away. "What do we do now?"

"We look for stairs," said Rosemary.

They were in a narrow, dim corridor. Around them, the jet buttons glittered like eyes.

"But this place could be full of ..." Peter waved his hands. "Anything! What do we do?"

"Calm down. It's going to be okay."

He frowned at her. "How do you know?"

"It's just a feeling."

"But —" Peter began, but Puck cut him off.

"What did I tell you about her instinct?" said Puck. "Sage Rosemary, where do you think we should go next?"

She looked up and down the corridor and pointed. They set off. The green carpeting was soft as moss; the only sound they could hear was the hiss of the gas lamps. The corridor stretched to a bend, offering no doors to rooms where danger could hide, but no place for them to hide, either, should danger strike. Turning the corner, they saw the corridor continue, with no doors, to another bend.

After ten minutes of creeping in silence, they had turned several corners, and the corridor still continued on.

"Maybe we've gone in circles," said Peter.

"No," said Rosemary. "I've been counting. Right turn, then left, then right, then left. If the hallway is straight, it can't have turned back on itself."

They crept forward. The gaslights hissed. The floorboards creaked.

Rosemary stopped as she passed another turn. "This could go on forever."

"Maybe we should go back," said Peter.

"Hello!" Puck bellowed. Peter jumped out of his skin.

"Puck!" Rosemary clutched her chest. "What are you doing?!"

But Puck was undaunted. "Hello!" he shouted, cupping his hands to his mouth. "Whoever is here to challenge us, we await you!"

Peter pulled at his arm. "Are you sure about this?"

"Which would you rather face? The challenge, or this wretched wandering?"

Peter shook his head. "I don't know anymore!"

Then the lights dimmed. A breeze plucked at their clothes and whistled in the hollow spaces.

"Wandering!" said Peter. "Definitely going to go for the wandering!"

Rosemary grabbed his hand. "Come on!" They marched along the corridor. Turning the next corner, they stopped dead.

A spectre floated before them.

It was a translucent skeleton, clothed in wretched rags and dangling chains. It let out a moan that echoed through the corridor. It turned and floated towards them.

"Let's get out of here!" Peter gasped.

Rosemary tightened her grip on his hand. "No!"

He tried to pull free. "Rosemary, please, for the love of —"

She grabbed his arm with her other hand. "No, Peter. Think about it! Where would we run to?"

Puck placed a hand on Peter's shoulder. "Courage, Peter."

The spectre moaned as it gathered speed along the long hallway. Peter closed his eyes. Rosemary pulled him closer. The moan rose to a wail as the creature approached. Cold washed over them.

Then it was gone. The lights brightened. The corridor was silent. They were alone in the hallway.

"How did you know?" Peter croaked.

Rosemary still held tight to his arm and her voice shook, but she said, "I read these two books with haunted houses in them. I finished one, and I think this is it. Thank God it wasn't the other one." She shivered. "I'm pretty sure I know this story."

"Pretty sure?" Peter echoed.

"It was, like, four years ago!" She let go and stepped along the corridor to the next bend. "Hey!" she said, brightening. "Stairs!"

Peter and Puck stepped forward and looked. This corridor ended in a flight of stairs, leading up.

Rosemary narrowed her eyes. "Let's get to the bottom of this!"

"Or the top, as it were," Puck muttered. They strode up the stairs.

They came out into a ballroom. A crystal chandelier hung from the ceiling and mirrors lined the walls. The gaslight bounced and bounced again, and Peter and Rosemary had to stand still and blink. Puck seemed to have the eyes of a cat and was already making faces in the mirrors. Suits of armour stood in the corners, holding tall axes.

The floor beneath them began to shake. The gaslights on the chandelier flickered. The floorboards creaked. Around them, a spectral moan rose out of nowhere and tickled their spines.

"Stop it!" Rosemary shouted. "I've had enough of this!"

The shaking floor intensified into a rumble. The chandelier swung and tinkled like a wind chime. "This is a trick!" she yelled. "The house is mechanical!"

"The controls must be around somewhere!" shouted Peter.

"Let's find them!" Rosemary stumbled towards the fireplace. She jumped back as the flames leapt out at her. "Here! It's around here!" A portrait hung above the mantel. In the painting, the eyes of a stern white-haired man glared at her. Rosemary shifted her position, and the eyes followed her.

Darting to the mantel, Rosemary climbed the stonework and perched precariously. She raised her hand, two fingers sticking out, and poked the portrait hard in the eyes.

There was a scream from within.

Rosemary punched and her fist crashed through the canvas. Grabbing an edge, she began to tear the painting away.

The floor stopped shaking and the noises were silenced abruptly. Behind the portrait, somebody yelled, "Hey! Stop! That's valuable, that is!"

Peter rushed over and helped to pull the canvas away. Behind it they found an alcove filled with mechanical equipment. A short man sat on a stool by the controls, clutching his eyes.

Peter jumped into the alcove and grabbed the man's swivel chair. "Who are you?"

The man swung around. He was wearing a snarling, gap-toothed witch doctor mask. "Yah!" He lunged at Peter.

Peter stumbled out of the alcove, fell off the mantel, and landed on the floor.

CHAPTER EIGHT

MIRROR, MIRROR

"She will."

— Marjorie Campbell

The man leapt off the mantelpiece and pulled off his mask. He pointed at Peter and cackled. "Got you!"

He was a small man with a round, red face like a cherub, but his eyes were as dark as holes.

Keeping her eye on the little man, Rosemary climbed down while Puck helped Peter to his feet. "You run this place?" Rosemary asked.

The man tapped his fingers together and gave her a little bow. "Actually, Miss Watson, I am filling in for the proprietor. You remember old Professor Herman?"

The light dawned. "Yes! Professor Herman!"

"Huh?" said Peter.

"This old guy who rigged the house to move around and make noises to scare everybody away," said Rosemary. "But two kids weren't scared off; they made friends with him and got him back into the real world."

"They just left the house behind at the end of the story," said the man. "They didn't tell you whether they shut it down or not, so it's still here, and I'm able to make use of it."

"Why?" demanded Peter, still brushing himself off. "Why did you try to scare us like that?"

"So, I *did* scare you?" said the little man eagerly.

"Yes!"

The man clapped and bounced on the balls of his feet. "Oh, good, good, good! I do so love a job well done!"

"This is your job?" said Rosemary.

"My life, actually," said the man. "I'm sorry, haven't I introduced myself? I am the Fearmonger, and fear is my life."

"The Fearmonger?" echoed Rosemary.

"I — I've never read about a Fearmonger," said Peter.

"I am not a character," the Fearmonger bubbled, "but I am in most works of fiction." He threw his arms wide. "I am the shadow in the corner! I am the ghost that lurks in dark alcoves! I am the twitching doorknob on an unlocked door. Fear is my service to the Land of Fiction."

"Some service," snapped Peter, "scaring people out of their wits!" He turned and was suddenly face to face with a living, breathing gargoyle. Its stone tongue lolled.

"Yah!" said the gargoyle.

Peter stumbled back, tripped, and fell to the floor.

The Fearmonger tossed the mask aside. "Got you again!"

Rosemary eyed the Fearmonger and his cheeky grin. "You're enjoying this!"

"And so are you," said the Fearmonger. "Look at yourself, Miss Watson: your heart is still beating at twenty percent over its normal rate after your trip through the corridor and your skin is delightfully flushed. How do you feel? Alert, I'll wager. Excited? Invigorated?"

Despite herself, Rosemary grinned. "Yeah, it was kind of fun."

"Well, I'm not having fun," muttered Peter from the floor. Rosemary gave him a guilty glance.

"I am glad I could be of service," said the Fearmonger. "It is my duty, after all, to test your mettle. Only if you pass me will you be worthy to save your brother, Theo."

Peter stood up. Rosemary stared at the Fearmonger, wide-eyed.

"Yes, I have followed your every step, Miss Watson," the Fearmonger continued. "I must say, I am impressed with your performance so far. I had never realized what a brave young person you were."

"Well, I have to be," said Rosemary. "Theo's my brother. This is not some book!"

"Indeed it is not some book." The Fearmonger began to pace, making slow, measured strides as he strolled around them, his heels clicking on the marble floor. "But I know you, Miss Watson. I've looked out at you from almost every book you've read. You do not do well with books."

Rosemary shivered. The room was suddenly colder.

"And now you hunt for the characters who kidnapped your brother — you, yourself, not some figure on the page. You face the risks, now, the terms. And to think of what you face; why, it would make me quake in my boots!"

Rosemary couldn't get warm. "Wh-what am I facing?"

He came close and whispered over her shoulder. "Only your worst fears."

She stared at him.

He circled again. "I know you, Miss Watson. I know that, for every four novels you start, three go unfinished. Two get tossed against the wall."

His footsteps grew heavier. The Fearmonger was taller, now, and getting taller with every step. Peter stood horrified. Puck looked on in silence, his arms folded and his face grim. And it was so *cold*.

"*You* are fighting these things, Miss Watson," the Fearmonger purred, his voice now an octave deeper. "Only, you can't throw the book down and run away. It will be you falling into the volcano, you facing execution at dawn, you trapped in the tomb, in the dark, with nothing but scarab beetles for company."

Rosemary clutched her arms around herself to try to keep from quaking.

Peter struggled out of his trance and grabbed her shoulder. "Rosemary, don't listen to him!"

She could hardly hear him. She couldn't answer. He turned her around and shouted into her face. "Rosemary! He's trying to scare you off!"

The Fearmonger leapt at Peter, his face transformed into the face of a snarling wolf. Peter scrambled back.

The Fearmonger pulled off his mask. "Got you a third time!" Then he turned back to Rosemary, leaned over her shoulder, and began whispering into her ear like a bad conscience. "How will you fight, Miss Watson? You have no weapons. How will you face creatures that can fold themselves out of sight? Who will protect you?"

Her gaze shifted up and settled upon Peter.

The Fearmonger chuckled. "The boy? He ran as though ten knights were after him, not just one. What else do you have?"

Rosemary looked at Puck. The Fearmonger followed her gaze. His smile didn't falter. "You? What can you do to help her?"

Puck smiled and then transformed into a wolf, snarling like the Fearmonger's mask. Rosemary ducked as he leapt at the Fearmonger.

With a yell of terror, the Fearmonger bolted. He ran. Peter tripped him, and he went down heavily.

Rubber masks of all varieties, from ghouls to dentists, burst from the Fearmonger's coat and skidded across the floor. He cowered as the wolf whirled around, transformed back into Puck, and stood there tapping his foot.

"Got you!" said Puck.

Peter and Rosemary burst out laughing.

The Fearmonger scowled. "That wasn't funny!" But he couldn't stop Peter and Rosemary from doubling over with laughter. "Stop it!" he yelled, his voice rising in anger. "Stop laughing at me!"

Rosemary, still giggling, glanced at the Fearmonger. Then she stared in astonishment.

He had been barely five feet tall when she'd first seen him. He was six feet tall when he was circling her. Now he was shorter than her sister Trisha. And he was still shrinking.

As Rosemary and Peter watched, the Fearmonger jumped up and down in fury. "See what you've done!" he squeaked.

"What's happened to you?" asked Rosemary. She started to laugh again.

"It is your laughter, Rosemary," said Puck. "Laughter is an excellent way to reduce one's fear." He picked up the doll-sized Fearmonger and held him at arm's length. "Now then, little man. How do we leave this house?"

The Fearmonger folded his arms. "I won't tell you."

Puck took a deep breath and said, "A knight, a monk, and a donkey walk into an inn —"

"Stop!" the Fearmonger shrieked. "Okay, okay, I'll let you out!" He grumbled as Puck set him down. "Pesky kids!"

Peter folded his arms. "The way out?"

The Fearmonger climbed up the mantel and into the alcove. He pressed a button on the controls. Two doors at the end of the hall, camouflaged by mirrors, opened.

Rosemary smiled grimly. "Thank you."

"You'll be sorry!" the Fearmonger shouted. "You can't stop yourself from being afraid, and when you fear, you'll face me again!"

"Yeah, whatever," said Peter.

"And I'll be taller!"

They headed for the doors. Halfway, Rosemary caught movement at the corner of her eye and whirled. She found herself face to face with her own reflection in one of the mirrored walls.

"What is it?" asked Peter.

"Nothing. It was just my" — she paused — "reflection?"

A girl looked back and raised her hand as Rosemary raised hers. Rosemary frowned. Her reflection smirked. Then, with a flick of her hands, the reflection changed the glasses she was wearing. The girl from the library stood before her.

Rosemary felt herself grabbed by invisible hands and tossed at the mirror. She closed her eyes and braced herself for the shattering impact, but felt instead a brief flash of cold, like passing through a thin waterfall, and found herself on the marble floor.

"Rosemary!" Peter shouted behind her. His voice sounded as if it had come from behind glass. She turned, and saw Peter standing in a mirror behind her, fists thumping against the surface. The room around her was different, darker and backwards.

"I said you'd be sorry!" the Fearmonger shouted as he frantically stuffed his full-sized masks into his pint-sized pockets. "You've incurred Her wrath! I'm leaving. You are all done for!" He disappeared down the stairs.

"Her?" Rosemary echoed. Then she turned around. She gasped as she bumped into the girl.

The girl grabbed Rosemary by the throat.

"Do you remember?" said the sandpaper voice.

"Remember what?" Rosemary choked.

"Do you remember the books?" said the girl.

"I don't — *gaak!* — I don't know what you're talking about!"

"The three out of the four?" the girl whispered. "No? Then remember this!" She shoved Rosemary to the floor and laughed as she ran into the darkness.

Rosemary sat alone in the darkened room. Her breath echoed around her. The shadows were far from empty. As she listened, other sounds started to be heard above the blood rushing in her ears and the muffled sounds of Peter and Puck's frantic discussions of where she had gone and how to get her back.

"I know this place." Her voice echoed. She drew her arms around herself. "I know this place!"

She scrambled to her feet and ran back to the mirror Peter was beating against. Puck was behind him, watching nervously.

Rosemary felt the mirror. It was solid glass. She laid her hand to match Peter's, but felt nothing. "Puck, what happened?" she called. "Is this another challenge?"

"No!" His voice was muted. "The Fearmonger was the test and he has just fled."

"What happened? Why am I alone?"

The word echoed in her mind. *Alone.*

Or was the echo just in her mind?

A breeze rushed through the house, thrumming through the hallways, like rooms exhaling. In a distant wing, a deep beat began, like a huge drum being struck repeatedly, or a giant marching to war.

Rosemary tried not to breathe fast. "There's got to be a way out of this! That makes sense, right? They got me in, they have to be able to get me out, right?"

Peter looked at her. "Rosemary, I —"

"Just say 'right!'" She felt around the mirror for switches, catches, anything.

The drumming footsteps continued to echo through the house. Rosemary shot a look at Peter. His hands were growing white as he pushed desperately at the glass.

The booming rhythm drew closer. Rosemary thought she saw the ceiling shudder under the weight of some presence above her. Then the sound travelled away, but came down a level. The floor began to shake to the beat of it.

Then the drumbeat stopped.

A noise closer made Rosemary whirl around.

A light was shining beneath a door leading out of the room. Something was moving in front of the light. A shadow flickered across the foot of the door. Something was sniffing for an opening, grunting and growling like an animal, or something worse than an animal.

Rosemary swallowed hard. "Peter?"

At the sound of her voice, the shadow jerked. The grunts increased in intensity. The doorknob jiggled and then began to turn.

Puck was staring through another mirror, examining the edges carefully, and frowning. Peter was saying, "I — I can't get through to her. It's all solid glass!"

Rosemary backed into her mirror. "Peter? Puck? Get me out of here!"

The doorknob slipped, then jiggled again. The grunts behind the door came quicker, became frustrated.

Then there was a fearsome shriek as the creature threw itself at the doors. The crash echoed through the room. The heavy oak panels bulged inward under the assault, twisting like rubber.

Rosemary whirled back and thumped the mirror. "Peter! Get me out! Something's in here with me!"

Puck marched over to a suit of armour and yanked an axe free. The armour jangled into a pile of parts. Puck handed the axe to Peter. "Get her out."

Peter hefted the axe and aimed for the mirror. Then he hesitated. "What if I hurt Rosemary?"

"That is a risk you will have to take, boy," said Puck. "Do it!"

In the reflected room, the door burst open. With a guttural snarl, something bounded through.

"Peter!" Rosemary screamed.

Closing his eyes, Peter swung the axe into the glass. Rosemary broke into a million pieces.

Then she found herself outside the mirror, on the floor, gasping. She was surrounded by little pieces of glass: little pieces of the girl's face, laughing at her. She scrambled to her feet. Peter caught her with one arm. He was still holding the axe. "Are you okay?"

"Sage Rosemary," said Puck. "Do not be afraid. You are free now."

Rosemary stared at the mirrors. She raised her hand and pointed. Peter and Puck looked.

The mirrors surrounded them with angry faces. People glared in from every glass, people of all ages, all shapes and sizes, in all forms of dress. There was a woman in a torn dress that used to be elegant, a boy with a black eye, and more.

Then they heard a scream from behind them. "Rosemary, help me!"

Rosemary whirled around.

Framed in the mirror was a young woman of around twenty. Her blue-green taffeta was torn and her blonde hair was tumbling from its bun. She beat against the mirror. "Let me out! For the love of God, let me out! Something's in here with me!"

"It's Lydia!" Rosemary rushed forward. "We've got to help her!"

Puck grabbed her and held her back. "No. Remember the princess!"

From behind Lydia there came the sound of a grunting animal. She whirled around and pressed her back to the mirror. "No! Keep away from me! Keep away!" Then something lashed out and pulled her from view. Peter winced and Rosemary buried her face in Puck's tunic as the screams and the animal snarls rang through the room.

"We should have helped her!" Rosemary sobbed.

"It was a trap," said Puck, his hands in her hair. "It is still a trap."

The figures in the mirrors turned so that they faced away from the ballroom. They started to walk away. Rosemary frowned. Why would they be walking away?

Then a thought jabbed her in the stomach. What if the mirrors were showing what was really in the room? In the mirrors, the characters were closing in on her reflection and the reflections of Peter and Puck. "We're under attack!"

Peter shivered. He gripped his axe. "I can't see them, but I can feel them. They're getting closer!"

Rosemary coughed. The smell of mildew clawed at her lungs.

Puck pulled Peter and Rosemary close to him. His voice rang out. "Attack a young maiden without even the courtesy of letting her see you? Are you not honourable characters?"

At once, the room was filled with angry whispers.

"Coward!"

"Abandoner!"

"No honour in her!"

"Revenge!"

Peter gulped. "You made them mad."

"I made nothing. They were already mad," Puck muttered. "Let us move to the doors. *I* can see these rogues, and there is still a pathway."

Rosemary glanced at the mirrors. The characters were almost in a circle around them, tracking them as they crept towards the doors.

"Get her!" whispered a voice.

Peter shot a look at the mirror and his eyes went wide. "Rosemary! Look out!" He lunged for her, swinging his axe. There was the sound of ripping paper, and two halves of a bear fell out of the air, its paws raised to claw.

Suddenly Rosemary rose into the air, choking. Peter looked to a mirror for some guidance but was knocked to the ground. Rosemary cried out as something struck her in the back of the head.

Puck rushed forward, transforming in a whirl of green and gold into a giant eagle. The bird's body was as big as Puck's had been, and its wings seemed to fill the room. The great talons struck at whatever was holding Rosemary. She crumpled and lay on the floor in a daze.

The eagle swept its huge wings forward, scattering their invisible foes with audible crashes. But in the mirror, Lydia stepped behind Puck and raised a fireplace poker.

Peter shouted a warning, but it was too late. The poker hit the eagle in the temple.

Puck gave a skirling cry and toppled out of the air, catching himself on human hands.

Peter scrambled up, swinging the axe. Around them, characters folded into existence, arms raised.

"Flee!" Puck cried. He gathered up Rosemary and stumbled for the door. Peter followed, staggering backward, swinging the axe to keep the folding people at bay.

At the last mirror in the ballroom, the girl in the horn-rimmed glasses tracked them as they darted past.

They burst through the back doors. Puck carried Rosemary out into the thunderstorm.

Behind them, steady in the buffeting winds, the Zeppelin hovered over the house.

CHAPTER NINE

THE MAGICAL MYSTERY TOUR

"No, don't hurt her!"
— Theo Watson

Rosemary dreamt of chrome and Zeppelins, of three children drinking cocoa from melamine cups.

* * *

"What if we could travel at the speed of thought?" Marjorie pushed her horn-rimmed glasses further up on her nose. "Wouldn't it be great? We could go anywhere, see all the planets, and not have to worry about spacesuits, rocket ships, and stuff."

"Yeah, right," snorted her brother, John. "You know, Marjorie, your flights of fancy are probably the reason the other kids think you're so weird."

"I don't think that's weird," said Andrew. "They used to think flying was impossible, or travelling around the world. Who knows? Maybe we could travel at the speed of thought in the future."

"Why not now?" said Marjorie.

Andrew looked at her. "Okay, maybe that is a little weird."

Marjorie scowled at him.

* * *

Rosemary's dream faded into a distant train whistle.

"Marjorie," murmured Rosemary. A light rocking and a whispered clickity-clack brought her slowly back to consciousness. She felt weak and warm. Somebody had covered her with a coat. She kept her eyes closed because she knew the world would tilt and reel the moment she opened them. Around her, voices whispered.

"Why did they attack us like that?" Peter's voice came from just over her head.

"To send us a message," said Puck, further off, "that they are angry."

Peter gave a hollow laugh. "That came through loud and clear."

"Angry enough they care not for the rules," Puck muttered. Then he perked up. "You seem troubled, young Peter."

"They tried to kill us!"

"It is more than that."

"Well ..." Peter said nothing for a moment. Rosemary realized that she was on her back on a cot or a long seat. Peter was sitting by her head. Finally, Peter said, "I — I think the Fearmonger was right."

"How so?"

"You saw how I ran when the Black Knight charged me! You saw how I was about to run when I saw that fake ghost! Some 'lady's champion' I turned out to be. I shouldn't even be here."

"And yet, when you saw Sage Rosemary threatened, you defended her without thought to your own safety."

"That's different. Rosemary was in trouble —"

"And you were not?"

Peter sat silent.

After a while, Puck said, "Fear, like strong medicine, is good in small doses. Running from the Black Knight was not cowardice, but common sense. What you did in the hall of mirrors, however, was true bravery."

"Well … I …" Peter glanced down at Rosemary. "I think she's coming around."

Rosemary opened her eyes. Her headache had disappeared and the world did not twirl around her. Much. "Where are we?"

"On a train." Peter helped her to sit up. A grey coat that had been over her like a blanket slipped to the floor. Rosemary found herself wearing a loose, straight dress of yellow silk with fringe on its knee-length hem. She kicked off the high-heeled shoes.

Peter's charcoal-coloured pants matched the coat and he had on a white pressed shirt. Puck wore the matching fedora cocked on his head; the bruise on his temple was not quite lost in its shadow.

Rosemary rubbed the last of the dizziness from her eyes. "Another challenge?" She looked around the compartment. There was a door on one side, its window opening onto the train car's corridor. On the other side, the countryside clattered past, scrubby fields rolling into the distance. "Where are we going?"

"Further into the story," Puck began.

"I'm talking about this train, not the story," snapped Rosemary.

"We didn't have time to ask," said Peter. "The characters were still chasing us. We saw this train and just piled on board."

"You don't know where we're going?" said Rosemary.

"The conductor said something about a Magical Mystery Tour."

"Magical Mystery Tour?" Rosemary raised both eyebrows.

"I know," said Peter. "We didn't get to ask him, and he hasn't come back to collect our tickets — which is actually good 'cause we don't have any."

Rosemary rubbed the back of her head, and then her sore neck. She winced at the sudden jab of pain and stopped rubbing. "Peter, do I have paper cuts …" She mimed grabbing her own throat.

Peter didn't meet her eyes. He nodded. She let her hand drop.

At the head of the train, the steam engine whistled again. Then they were in the darkness of a tunnel.

There was a sliding sound.

"Was that our compartment door?" asked Peter.

The train continued in the darkness.

"Peter," said Rosemary. "What's your hand doing on my knee?"

"My hand isn't on your knee."

The train chugged on. There was silence for a minute. Then, "Puck?"

"Yes?" His voice was across the compartment. Not beside her.

Beside Rosemary, somebody let out a baritone laugh. Pandemonium broke loose.

"There's someone here with us!" Rosemary shouted.

"Get away!" shouted Peter.

The intruder laughed again.

"He's choking me!" Peter croaked.

"I got him!" shouted Rosemary. "I got him by the neck!"

"Help!" Peter gurgled.

The train emerged from the tunnel. The sudden light revealed Puck standing up, staring, as Rosemary held Peter in a headlock. She dropped him, and he stumbled to his feet. They looked around at the otherwise empty compartment.

"I don't get it," said Peter. "Was somebody here?"

"Maybe," said a voice.

Peter and Rosemary jumped. They looked around frantically, but could see no one. "Who's there?" Rosemary's voice shook. "Where are you?"

"Who indeed?" said the voice. "Where do you think?"

Then movement caught her eye and she found herself staring at the window. The light twisted atop the seat, and she could just make out the shape of a tall man made out of clear glass. She gripped Peter's wrist and pointed. The two backed into Puck.

"Wh-what are you doing here?" said Peter.

The transparent figure turned. They could see the shape of his hat brim as it bent the light from the window. "Don't you know?" They couldn't see if his lips had moved or not.

Puck put a protective hand on Peter's and Rosemary's shoulders. "Will you not answer the children's questions?"

The figure folded his invisible arms. "Can't they figure things out for themselves?"

"No," said Rosemary. "We've never seen you before — we can hardly see you at all! We don't know who you are or what you want! Do you have to be so mysterious?"

"Maybe."

"Wait," said Peter. "You *have* to be so mysterious."

The man stood up. "Yes, that's right, Peter. It's my nature. I am made of mystery. I am the Mystery Man!"

Rosemary and Peter looked at each other. "So, what are you doing here?" asked Rosemary.

"What do you think?"

"I don't want to think!" Rosemary shouted. "I'm too tired to think! I just want answers!"

"You are here to help us, though," said Peter.

The Mystery Man cocked his head, causing the wood panelling behind him to ripple. "What makes you think so?"

"Well," said Peter. He eased out of Puck's protective grip and stepped forward. "You haven't attacked us. Scared us, yes, and confused us, but you haven't tried to hurt us."

"That is thin evidence," said the Mystery Man, "but evidence enough to form a theory. Well done, Peter. You're starting to use your mind."

Rosemary scowled. "If you're here to help, why don't you just say so?"

Puck tapped her shoulder. "Be easy, Rosemary. Peter has found a pattern. Use it, and you can talk to this man."

She frowned up at him. "What do you mean?"

"I think I understand," said Peter. "Let me try again." He turned to the transparent figure. "You want to help us, but … you can't give much away. We have to figure things out ourselves through the clues you provide."

"And your evidence?" said the Mystery Man.

"You never answer our questions," said Peter. "You make us guess, and only tell us if we're right or wrong."

"Very good."

"You're the reason why they called this train the Magical Mystery Tour," said Rosemary, brightening.

"Very good, Rosemary," said the man. "It isn't too hard, once you get started, to use your mind."

"But why would you be here on a train?" she asked.

"Why do you think?"

Rosemary clenched her fists and growled.

"There's something special about this train," said Peter. "Something to do with mysteries."

"Trains can offer glamorous and contained settings, a limited number of suspects, and a time limit for the mystery to be solved. I am very much at home on a train."

"The Magical Mystery Tour," said Rosemary. "I don't know the magical part, but you're the mystery, and then there's 'tour.' Here we can tour mysteries. If you're the Mystery Man, and mystery is your life, then this train must be full of mysteries!"

The Mystery Man clapped like balloons breaking. "I know you haven't read many of my books, Rosemary," he said, "but I knew you'd do well. You have a strong mind, and a strong intuition. A formidable combination."

Rosemary blushed.

"There are mysteries all over this train?" asked Peter. "Can we see them?"

"What do you think?" said the man.

"That wasn't a question, that was a request," said Peter.

"Ah." The Mystery Man chuckled. He stepped around them to the compartment door. "Follow me. Every compartment on this train does indeed have a mystery afoot. Even this one, if you look hard enough. Let me show you some others."

They followed his footprints into the corridor, walking in single file as the countryside streamed past. They stopped at the next compartment, peering through the glass partition.

One woman was slumped in her seat, crying. Three other adults, two men and one younger woman, shifted uncomfortably in their seats. All were dressed in the same style as Peter and Rosemary.

Standing in the middle of the compartment were two teenagers, a boy and a girl. They were blond and dimpled and dressed to match; they looked like salt and pepper shakers. They were questioning the younger woman, pointing accusing fingers as she protested her innocence.

"What do you think happened here?" asked the Mystery Man.

"Um ... nobody's happy," said Peter. "I don't know —"

"The crying woman's lost her necklace," said Rosemary.

The Mystery Man turned to her. "How do you know?"

"Both women are wearing lots of jewellery," said Rosemary, "but the one who's crying doesn't have a necklace. I — I think she accused the others of stealing it."

"Very good," said the Mystery Man. "What do you think has happened to the necklace?"

"That's what the two detectives are trying to find out," said Rosemary.

"Aren't they a little young to be detectives?" said Peter.

"Well, I've read plenty of books about young detect—" Rosemary stopped short and took another look inside the compartment. Then she pulled open the door and burst in. "Nicholas! Eleanor! Tell her to look in her luggage again!"

The two teenagers looked at her in astonishment. Then the boy's face brightened in recognition. "Rosemary? Is that you?"

Eleanor's eyes widened. "Rosemary? How many years has it been?"

"Never mind that," said Rosemary. "The luggage. Have her look!"

The crying woman hauled her suitcase from beneath her seat. "All right, I'll have another look, but I'm telling you —" She stopped short. "Here it is! It must have fallen out of its case! Thank you!" She hugged first the boy and then the girl before putting the necklace on. To the adults, she said, "I am sorry I accused you of stealing. No hard feelings?"

Nicholas and Eleanor followed Rosemary out into the corridor. "You know these two?" Peter asked Rosemary.

"Yes," said Rosemary. "Peter, Puck, meet Nicholas and Eleanor Jung, the Jung detectives!"

Nicholas and Eleanor greeted everybody with warm handshakes. When they were all introduced, Nicholas gave the Mystery Man a sour look. "You said we'd have a real mystery."

"Wasn't that a mystery?" asked the Mystery Man. "Didn't you find the missing necklace?"

"You call that a mystery?" said Eleanor. "We want something more serious!"

"More exciting!" said Nicholas.

"With bodies!" said Eleanor.

"What do you mean?" asked Rosemary.

"We didn't solve a murder, prevent blackmail, foil burglars, or anything," said Nicholas. "We haven't had a real mystery. We never have real mysteries!"

"But what about the Dashenberg Diamond?" asked Rosemary. "You solved the Mystery of the Wailing Catacombs!"

"A racoon with an eye for shiny things! A lost cat in an empty crypt!" said Eleanor.

"Still mysteries," said the Mystery Man. "You find a question and, through research and investigation, you answer it. Archeologists are among the best detectives in the world, and they lead quiet lives — most of them."

"And what of life's mysteries?" said Puck. "Who are we and how came we to be here? Solving those questions will bring you no fame."

"We know we can solve mysteries," said Eleanor sourly. "We've solved twenty-three cases, but we want excitement too! We want a thriller! We want bodies!"

"Why would you want such a thing?" asked Puck.

"We get all the boring stuff because we're children," said Nicholas.

"Everybody else has bodies," said Eleanor. "Look." She motioned them to the next compartment.

Rosemary looked in through the glass partition. She covered her mouth.

Inside, a body lay in the centre of the compartment, laced with stab wounds, some glancing, some deep. His dead eyes stared and his mouth lolled open. Around him, four people shifted in their seats as a bald, round-headed detective fiddled with his handkerchief before launching into his theory of how the murder happened.

"We can solve mysteries as well as the grown-ups," said Eleanor. She cast a glance inside. "If you want my opinion on this one, all of them did it. But do we get asked? No. And why? Because we don't have foreign accents or smoke pipes, and why should we? We're from Kennebunkport and our parents won't let us take up smoking!"

"It's a filthy habit anyway," said Nicholas.

"All of them did do it," said Rosemary under her breath.

"What?" Everybody looked at her.

"Well, yes," said Eleanor. "If you look at the wounds, you will see that the knife blows came from different angles, some left-handed, some right. Of course most people would think there was only one murderer, but once you get past that, you will see that they might all have killed him together —"

"They did," said Rosemary. "They hated him. He did bad things to them. They wanted revenge, and they got it." She shivered.

The others stared at her.

"Yes," said the Mystery Man finally. "Most interesting, Rosemary." He took her hand gently. "Come have a look at this." He led her to the next compartment. Rosemary looked inside and gasped.

Two women in Edwardian dresses sat in the compartment. One woman, pale-skinned and dark-haired, was clearly upset. She was being questioned by a police officer in an old-style London uniform. A man in a deerstalker hat lounged in the corner, watching everything but saying nothing.

The other woman, with darker skin and flaming red hair, was dead. Blood trickled down from a hole just above her right temple. The left part of her head was —

Rosemary's hand flew to her mouth. She turned away from the compartment window.

Nicholas peered in, frowning. "The policeman's on the wrong track. He's accusing her of the murder. Just because you see the one suspect doesn't mean that no more exist."

"The dead woman killed herself." Rosemary's voice shook. "She thought the other woman was having an affair with her husband. She's trying to frame the other woman for a murder! She tied a gun to a rock or something so she could shoot herself in the head and it would fly out the window."

Eleanor looked into the compartment. "Good theory! The other woman would have to be pretty stupid to leave herself as the only suspect."

The man in the deerstalker hat raised his head and looked at Rosemary. She drew her arms around herself and quaked.

"What's going on?" Peter whispered to Puck. "She couldn't figure out the Mystery Man, but she's solved every mystery she's looked at. How does she know all this?"

Puck grinned. "It's a mystery!"

"Yes, I said there was a mystery in every compartment," said the Mystery Man. "Even yours. Rosemary is that mystery."

"Rosemary, what's wrong?" said Nicholas. "You're as white as a sheet!"

"Have you thought about taking up sleuthing?" asked Eleanor. "Assuming the Mystery Man considers you old enough for bodies, of course."

"Stop it!" Rosemary burst into tears. "Don't you care about these people? Don't you have any idea how they suffered?"

Peter frowned. "Rosemary, they're just characters!"

"There is nothing 'just' about being a character!" Rosemary yelled. "Characters are born, they grow old, they fall in love, and they die! We are born, we grow old, we fall in love, and we die! What's the difference?"

"B-but Rosemary," said Peter, "they're not people!"

"To me they are! I can *feel* them!"

Puck took Rosemary's hand gently and pulled her away from the compartment. "I have always wondered why Rosemary could not finish most of her books," he said. "And now I know. Sage Rosemary, how did you forgive me for turning Bottom's head into that of an ass?"

Rosemary smiled wanly. "He *was* an ass," she said. "And I knew that it wasn't going to be permanent."

"No one gets hurt in *A Midsummer's Night Dream*," said Peter. "In a couple of years we'll have *Romeo and Juliet*. I think that's going to be a problem. But I don't understand; if Rosemary hates to see these characters suffer, why are they attacking her?"

"Just get me out of here," Rosemary muttered. "Please?"

The Mystery Man nodded, his transparent hat brim shimmering the air. "She can't stay on this train. It would be too much for her."

"Come on," said Peter, taking her by the shoulders and leading her back to their compartment. There, he slid open the door.

Rosemary stepped inside, looked up, and screamed.

A girl's body dangled from the ceiling. "Oh, my God!" Peter pulled Rosemary out into the corridor. "Puck! There's a body in our compartment!"

Nicholas and Eleanor perked up. "A body in their compartment?" They glanced at each other and broke into grins. "There's a body in their compartment!" They rushed forward, but stopped short at the compartment door. They looked up and went pale.

Nicholas fainted. Gagging, Eleanor ran for the bathroom, holding her mouth closed.

Peter and Puck stared up at a girl very like Rosemary, her head lolling above a noose. She swung gently in time to the clickity-clack of the wheels over the rails.

Rosemary covered her eyes. She leaned against the opposite wall.

The Mystery Man stepped inside the compartment, looking up at the body. "This isn't supposed to be here."

"Look!" Peter inched past the dangling feet and peered out the window.

Puck followed him in. "Peter, what do you see?"

Peter was glued to the window. "That Zeppelin is back."

Behind their backs, the hanging corpse raised its head and glared at Rosemary through its horn-rimmed glasses.

"You're next," the dead girl mouthed.

Puck pointed. "Wait. That shadow, by our own; that does not belong to the skyship."

Peter craned his neck up. "There's another Zeppelin."

The window shattered inward. Peter scrambled back. A grapple slid into the compartment, grabbing at the air like a three-fingered claw.

The train shook. The door slid closed.

The man in the deerstalker hat leapt into the passageway and grabbed Rosemary from behind.

The hanging girl grabbed the noose, loosened it, and jumped on Peter, knocking him to the compartment floor.

Rosemary struggled, yelling, but her attacker wrestled her down and pressed his forearm to her throat. His clothes were wet and heavy. She choked. Her eyes widened as he pulled a double-hypodermic needle from his pocket, a murder weapon whose mark had masqueraded as a snakebite. The twin tips dripped with poison.

"Let her go!" Eleanor ran back from the bathroom and jumped on the man's back. He struggled and elbowed the girl, hard. Rosemary punched desperately. Her right arm, still blackened from its dip in the Sea of Ink, landed solidly in the man's stomach. He grunted. His grip slacked.

Nicholas, staggering up, tried to shove open the compartment door.

Inside, Puck and the Mystery Man pulled the flailing girl off of Peter.

The man in the deerstalker hat knocked Eleanor off him and dragged Rosemary to her feet. He held her from behind and pressed the hypodermic to her throat as Puck, Peter, and the Mystery Man poured out of the compartment.

"Do not move!" he shouted, his voice rich and British. "We are taking her! We shall have our revenge!"

The girl with the horn-rimmed glasses stepped to the door of the compartment. "Now!"

The man in the deerstalker hat shoved Rosemary into a window. It caved in. Rosemary screamed as a grapple caught her blackened arm in its metal teeth.

Peter and Puck rushed forward, grabbing at the metal jaws, but they held fast. The man in the deerstalker hat moved to stop them, but the Mystery Man surged forward and blocked him like a wave of water. "Get off my train!" he shouted. They fought. The Mystery Man swept him back into the compartment.

The hook pulled back, dragging Rosemary towards the broken window.

"No!" Rosemary yelled. She flailed. The grapple holding her arm hit the wall and sprang open. She fell away and lay on the floor, moaning. Peter grabbed her arm to check for injuries. She wasn't even bleeding.

The Mystery Man emerged from the compartment, locking its door.

"How fast are these Zeppelins?" Peter gasped.

"As fast as the story requires," said the Mystery Man.

The grapple made another swing, but checked itself. The train pulled ahead. Peter could see the bulk of the Zeppelin above them edging into view. "Why are they hanging back?"

"We've entered a range of mountains and there's a tunnel ahead," said the Mystery Man.

"Tunnel?" said Peter. He peered out the hole in the side of the train as Puck helped Rosemary to her feet.

144

"Puck, I've got an idea!"

"I hope it's a good idea," said Eleanor. She held the door shut against the shouting and fists of the girl with the horn-rimmed glasses.

"We've got to get off this train," said Peter. "If we don't, the Zeppelins will keep following us and pick us off."

"But if you stop the train, we'll be sitting ducks," said Nicholas.

"Not the whole train," said Peter. "Just the last car."

"And use us as decoys!" exclaimed Eleanor. "Oh, how exciting!"

"You two" — the Mystery Man pointed at Nicholas and Eleanor — "hold these characters here. The rest of you, follow me!"

Pushing Rosemary ahead of them, Peter and Puck dashed along the corridors to the rear of the car. They pulled open the door to the next car and ran through that and through the one after that until they reached the end of the train.

At the entrance to the last car, they halted.

"We need to clear this car," said the Mystery Man. "Fast."

"I saw the murderer!" Peter shouted. "He went that way!" He pointed.

Heads poked out of the doors of the compartments. At the sight of Peter pointing, they stampeded into the corridor. Puck and Rosemary barely managed to duck away in time.

The Mystery Man took out a key and opened a panel. "Once you lose the Zeppelins, try to follow the train. We were heading towards the next setting."

"But then the Zeppelins will be between us and it," said Rosemary. "How do we get past them?"

"Let me deal with that," said Puck. "Your business is with the challenges."

The car plunged into darkness as they entered the tunnel. Puck moved Peter and Rosemary into the car, while the Mystery Man held back.

"Challenges are never easy, Rosemary. But it is from challenges that heroes are born." In the dying light, the Mystery Man pulled a lever. There was a rush of escaping air, and then the last car pulled back from the rest of the train, slowing steadily.

"Good luck, Miss Watson," said the Mystery Man. "You will save your brother, Theo." Then, bending the light from the corridor, he tipped his hat to them and waved.

Then the train pulled into the distance as the final car rolled to a stop.

"What now?" asked Rosemary.

"We walk," said Puck.

CHAPTER TEN

FALLING ACTION

"You heard the Wise Woman," said Marjorie, pushing her horn-rimmed glasses further up on her nose. "Anything is possible if we put our minds to it."

"Including jumping about the universe at a whim?" said John. "What do you take me for?"

"Just hold hands," Marjorie ordered.

"This is silly," said John, as Marjorie took Andrew's and John's hands into her own.

"Shh," said Andrew. "It can't hurt to try."

"You just like holding my sister's hand!"

There was a rushing of air. The world around them changed. Then there was a moment's stunned silence.

"Marjorie," said John, barely holding his voice steady.

"Oh dear," squeaked Marjorie. "It really does work!"

* * *

"Rosemary, are you okay?"

Rosemary snapped out of her daydream. "Yeah."

They trudged through the darkness of the tunnel, Rosemary stepping from tie to tie while Peter scuffed the rocks between the rails. As they came to the tunnel mouth, they crept close to the walls, keeping an eye on the sky, but there were no Zeppelins in view.

"I don't like this." Rosemary shivered. "They knew we were on that train."

"They're not here now," said Peter.

"When they see their error, they will come back to this tunnel with all speed." Puck craned his neck to see around the mountain.

"So, let's get out of here," said Peter. "Which way?"

"Perhaps that path is going our way." Puck pointed to a crossing ahead of them. The road clung to the side of the mountain, spiralling out of view.

"No cover," said Peter.

"Then keep one eye on the sky."

Peter and Rosemary puffed up the slope. The ledge narrowed, until all that was left was the roadway. The mountain was a sheer wall on their left and a sheer drop on their right.

As Rosemary limped along, Peter cast glances at her arm, still black from the Sea of Ink. Finally, he said, "Rosemary, is your arm okay?"

"Yeah, why?"

"How heavy was that grapple?"

"Heavy," said Rosemary.

"Didn't it hurt?"

"What do you think?"

"But you're okay now?"

"Yes, Peter, I'm okay. What are you getting at?" Puck raised one pointed eyebrow.

"That thing would have broken my arm," said Peter. "But you're okay?"

"Yes, Peter, I'm fine," she snapped. Then she winced and stumbled. "Ow!"

He looked down. "You're barefoot!"

"I'm wearing stockings."

"Like that makes a difference."

"Do you think those high-heeled shoes that went with this dress would help any? Anyway, I left them on the train."

"Why didn't you say anything?"

"You have shoes in your pockets?"

"Puck," Peter turned to him. "Could you change into a horse? Give us a ride?"

Puck snorted. "On these rocks? Would you ride a mountain goat?" He pointed. "Perhaps we can find shoes there."

"I'm fine," said Rosemary. She looked up. "Find shoes where?"

Ahead of them, the ledge widened. On it was a tall and narrow house. On top of a roof like a witch's hat a lightning rod waited for something to strike. The house was built right to the sheer drop.

Rosemary swallowed. "Guys, I'm fine."

"You can't walk around like this," said Peter, taking her hand. "Come on!"

In the shadow of the tall house amongst the barren rocks there was a little square of green. By the gate of this garden, an old man puttered around. Peter, Puck, and Rosemary walked up to him. "Excuse me, sir," said Peter. "Do you have any —"

The old man looked up and fixed Peter with eyes like planets. Peter froze.

The man was tall and thin, wearing flannel pants, a white shirt, and a waistcoat, all of which looked too formal for gardening. His hair was silver, and combed precisely. He ran his thumbs beneath his suspenders.

"What were you going to say, my boy, hmm?" said the old man, his voice crisp. "Shoes, was it? Shoes for young Rosemary Watson?"

"Uh, yeah," said Peter. He swallowed. "She hasn't got any."

"Really," said Rosemary. "I'm okay."

The old man beamed at her. "Nonsense! I would be remiss if I didn't look, my dear. I would be even more remiss if I didn't offer you my hospitality." He opened the gate. "Come in, come in! I've made you all some refreshments." He grabbed Peter's and Rosemary's hands and pulled them onto the lawn.

The cool grass felt wonderful to Rosemary's aching feet and she staggered at the rush of relief. She gazed longingly at a lawn chair beside a table that held a pitcher of lemonade and then shook herself, as though from a dream.

"Ooh, lemonade!" Peter started forward, but Rosemary grabbed his arm. She looked up at the old man. "How did you know I'd be coming?"

"It is my job to know these things. After all, I am the Professor."

"Professor what?" asked Peter.

"Oh, I'm much too busy to deal with names," said the Professor. Then he paused. "But I seem to recall my surname starts with the letter M. You may call me Professor Em, if you wish."

"What do you do, here, Professor Em?" asked Rosemary.

"Well, I'm afraid I control the forces of evil."

There was an uncomfortable silence. Finally, Peter said, "Well, at least you're honest about it."

"It is who I am," said the Professor. "And as for how I knew of your imminent arrival, let me show you something."

He beckoned Rosemary around the house, with the others following, and pointed to the wall. A bank of screens covered the expanse of brick. Some of the scenes she recognized, having passed through them, seemingly ages ago. At the base of the screen, a long console held keyboards, displays, and printouts.

"This is my control centre," said Professor Em. "My eyes and ears, the centre of my web, and all that." Something caught his attention and he turned to the screen. After a moment staring, he smiled, pressed a button, and spoke into an intercom. "Prince Valiant is heading down the path to the swamp. Cue the crocodiles!"

"Crocodiles!" cried Rosemary.

The Professor smiled at her. "I can't let him off easily. If he wants to rescue his fiancée from the quicksand, he's got to go through the crocodiles."

"His fiancée?" said Rosemary.

"Quicksand?" exclaimed Peter.

"You put his fiancée in quicksand?" said Rosemary.

"No, that was just bad luck," said the Professor. "But I arranged for his so-called friend to lead him into the crocodiles' path."

Rosemary stared at him, appalled.

"So, I have been watching you, Miss Watson," said the Professor. He tapped a screen that showed images of Rosemary at the beach before the Sea of Ink, at the bridge of the Black Knight, in the haunted house, and on the Magical Mystery Tour. "I knew you would come this way. I've met lots of heroes, you see. Speaking of which, are you hungry? Would you like a sandwich?"

Rosemary gave him a nervous glance. "No. Thank you."

The Professor smiled. "Never break bread with the enemy, eh? I suppose that's wise, but it's hardly civilized. Why don't you relax? Sit down. Talk with me. So few people do, and I appreciate the company."

The Professor's eyes were the colour of a pinstripe suit. Rosemary shivered. "No. W-we should be going."

"You've hardly rested," said the Professor. "You haven't even sat down. I haven't fetched new shoes. Come, have some lemonade. I made it myself."

"No, thanks," said Rosemary, backing away. "We really need to go, now."

"I worry you, don't I, Miss Watson?" said the Professor. "You think that I'll lead you into the path of the crocodiles as you attempt to rescue your brother."

"Well, wouldn't you?" said Peter.

"Of course," said the Professor. "But it would be for your own good. The truth is, you need me. You both need me."

Rosemary stopped. "I don't need you!"

"Certainly you do. Where would you be without me?"

"A lot happier!" said Peter.

"Are you sure about that? Are you really sure? Imagine, for a moment, a world without villains. Would you remember Robin Hood without the Sheriff? Superman in a perfect world? Behind every great hero is a great villain. Holmes had Moriarty. King Arthur had Morgaine. These legends would be nothing without their enemies."

"We're not talking about a book," said Rosemary. "We're talking about real life; we're talking about my brother!"

"Then let us consider real life," said the Professor. "Where would you be if not here, Miss Watson? Hiding in your study cubicle, I'd wager, reading your encyclopedias, running away from your books."

"Stop it!" Peter pulled Rosemary behind him. "We're leaving. You are not going to keep us here any longer."

Professor Em straightened up. His tongue, forked like a snake's, flicked out and tasted the air. "You're right, my boy. I've kept you here long enough."

There was a whine of engines, and out of the valley, three Zeppelins rose into view, taking their places in the sky. Their grapples dipped and weaved like dangling cobras.

"You tricked us!" Rosemary shouted.

The Professor shrugged. "My dear child, whatever did you expect?"

Rosemary could see the girl with the horn-rimmed glasses in the cockpit of one of the Zeppelins. The girl sneered at her.

"Ah, yes, there She is right now," said Professor Em. "This was Her idea. She is very new to the villain game, playing against type, in fact, but She has adapted. People do when they're angry."

The grapples lunged.

"Both of you, flee! I shall hold them off!" Puck picked up a stone the size of a soccer ball. He took three running steps and hurled it over his head. It sailed high and punched through the skin of the nearest Zeppelin. A hissing noise filled the air, and the Zeppelin sank out of view, its engines struggling and the cabin dropping ballast. Seconds later, there was a thump, and a fireball erupted skyward.

The other Zeppelins' engines surged, and they floated higher. The grapples descended, jaws open, and struck at Puck, who dodged.

Peter and Rosemary ran for the road, but the Professor flung his arms wide. They turned into tentacles and wrapped around Rosemary's and Peter's bodies. He hauled them back, their feet dangling in the air.

"What was it you read off the idea tree?" he said, his tongue flicking across Rosemary's cheek. "What if we could fly?"

"What if *rugs* could fly!" Rosemary cried, feet flailing. "Rugs!"

"Pity you don't have rugs, then. Bye-bye!" Peter and Rosemary screamed as he tossed them over the edge.

The girl with the horn-rimmed glasses came sliding down one of the grapple cables. She jumped to the ground and joined Professor Em at the cliff edge.

"Hey, you were supposed to capture them," she said. "Why did you throw them off the edge?"

"All the better to crunch their bones to make my bread. Have you ever tried to put unbroken bones through a grinder? Dear, dear, it is a bother!"

Rosemary fell. The tumbling air deafened her, carrying her screams away. Her hair whipped her face, and the long fringe of her dress lashed her arms and legs. Peter fell beside her, grey and unreadable as a shadow.

Suddenly she saw something plummet towards her, huge as a shark. It swooped past and swung beneath her, spreading tremendous wings.

Rosemary struck the eagle's back. It knocked the wind out of her. In her whirling vision, she saw Peter hit, and slide. She saw his pale hands pull out huge feathers. Then he fell again. "Puck!" she screamed.

"Hold fast!" the eagle cried. It folded its wings and dove after the falling boy. They passed Peter and swept under him. Rosemary dug her knees into Puck's back and caught hold of Peter's collar as he thudded and slid past. Peter grabbed desperately, plucking more feathers before steadying himself. He lay gasping. Rosemary held him.

His knuckles white, Peter looked back. "They're following us!"

"What do they want?" shouted Rosemary.

"To bring things to a head," said Puck. "They want to attack before you are ready. They are no longer interested in the story, only its climax."

"What do we do?" yelled Rosemary.

"Enough of challenges," said Puck. "I shall take you to the centre of the Land of Fiction, quick as I can."

He swooped close to the cliff face, turning a corner in the valley. The pursuing Zeppelin banked. "Where's the other one?" shouted Rosemary.

Then they turned another corner and found the second Zeppelin waiting for them.

It hovered at the rim of the valley, its sides almost touching either wall. It towered over them, eclipsing the sun. The grapple struck towards them.

"Hold on!" Puck screeched. He swerved down and right. Rosemary yelled. The wall of the valley swept towards them. The grapple was just feet behind. They were in the middle of a gap between grapple and cliff, and the gap was narrowing by the second.

The grapple swung in. Puck put on a burst of speed. The grapple hit the cliff face, raising a spray of rock and dust.

Then Puck's wing smashed against the cliff with a sickening crunch. Puck cried out and fell.

Rosemary and Peter clung for dear life against his back. The wind whistled in their ears. The ground rushed up to meet them.

"Look," Peter yelled, pointing. "The tracks!"

Rosemary looked ahead. Before them, the train tracks ran along a narrow ledge before crossing the valley on a high bridge, plunging into a tunnel.

Behind them, the second Zeppelin rose above the rim of the valley and began a ponderous turn. The first sailed past.

"Puck, slow down!" Rosemary cried.

"I can't!" Puck shouted. "My wing is broken!"

The ledge rushed towards them. Puck banked, his body shuddering. They were feet above the railway tracks, the gravel rushing past. "Jump!" he cried.

Peter grabbed Rosemary and rolled off Puck's back. They hit the ledge hard, rolling over and over.

Puck topped out and fell, hitting the tracks and cartwheeling. A cloud of dust rose up around him. When it cleared, they saw the eagle lying on its back, still. All was silent save for the drone of the Zeppelins.

Puck shuddered back into his accustomed body as Peter and Rosemary rushed to him. He clutched his arm, which was bent in a direction it wasn't supposed to go. His bright face was darkened with pain.

Rosemary knelt beside him, afraid to touch him. "Puck! Are you okay?"

He staggered to his feet. "No."

The drone of the Zeppelins grew louder as they tracked along the valley, grapples gnashing at thin air.

"You must cross the bridge," said Puck. "The quest leads there."

"We'd never make it," gasped Peter. "There's no way. They'll snatch us off the track!"

"I will make sure the path is clear," said Puck. He clasped Rosemary's shoulder with his good hand. "Brave Rosemary, you must go on."

Rosemary looked up. "What? Puck, what do you mean?"

He gave her a sad smile. "I must leave you."

"What? No! We can't go on without you!" She clutched at him.

He pried her off and touched her cheek. "I can no longer be your guide. But you are the hero. You must go on."

A shadow fell across them and they looked up. The Zeppelins were almost overhead.

Puck stepped back to the cliff edge. "Farewell."

Peter stood up. "What are you —"

Puck turned, took two staggering steps, and jumped off the edge.

Rosemary ran forward. "No!"

Puck flung his arms out and transformed back into a great golden eagle. He soared up with a sweep of his giant wings, even though one was broken. He turned his beak to the Zeppelin guarding the bridge and surged forward, faster and faster, becoming a blur, his feathers like fire.

Peter pulled Rosemary into the cliff face, shielding her with his body. The phoenix struck.

The Zeppelin burst. Shafts of flame shot out in all directions. The second Zeppelin caught and it too exploded.

Peter and Rosemary watched as the falling airships cracked against the railway bridge and crumbled. Their burning metal skeletons rained on the valley floor.

Puck was nowhere to be seen.

"Wow," said Peter. "Umm …" He struggled for words. Finally, "Wow."

Rosemary slumped down on the ground, curled up, and buried her face in her knees.

Chapter eleven

THE CITY OF MARBLE AND CHROME

The flames ebbed. The last piece of twisted metal top-pled off the bridge and echoed from the valley below. Then the only sound other than the flames licking on the bridge was the wind whistling through the canyon. Peter stood staring at the devastation, then looked at Rosemary, all curled up and rocking. He stood silent for several minutes, waiting for her to look up. She didn't.

Finally he reached out. "Hey." He touched her arm.

She swatted his hand away. "Leave me alone!"

He halted, stood a moment, then reached out again. "Hey."

She hit him harder. "I said leave me alone!"

He jerked back, then lunged forward and hauled her to her feet.

She beat at him. "Leave me alone!" Her words echoed through the canyon.

"Stop it." He grunted as a punch caught him across the mouth. "Ow!" He grabbed her wrists and shouted in her face. "Stop it!"

His words echoed back at them for several seconds. "Stop it! Stop it. Stop. Stop ..."

She stood in his grip, breathing hard. She didn't look at him.

"We have to keep going," he said, his voice level, firm.

"Why?" she said bitterly.

"Because he said so," he said. "He ..." He stumbled, cleared his throat, and took a deep breath. "You're the hero. He ... he did what he did so ... so that you could go on."

"What's the use?" Her eyes glistened. "We're no closer to finding Theo. Everything's attacking us, and the one person who could help us the most d-, d-, d-" She spat it out. "Dies!"

"It's —" Peter began. "We —"

"I shouldn't have come here!" Her voice echoed again. She struggled to free herself from his grip. "I shouldn't have brought you here! Now they're after you too!"

Peter's grip held firm. He looked at her levelly. "Let me guess. If this was a book, you'd have stopped reading right about now."

She stopped struggling. She looked at him.

"Well, it's not a book." He let go of her wrists and clasped her shoulders. "It's not going to go away just because you decide to stop. We've got to keep going."

"You go, then," she said, turning away. "Just leave me alone!"

"No!" he yelled, with such force that she jumped. "Not here, not now, not ever! Being alone is the worst thing in the world, and I'm not doing that to you. You didn't drag me here; you hit me over the head trying to stop me. But I came anyway! And now we're in this together, and we've got to work together if we want to get out! I'm not leaving this spot until you get that!"

Her face twisted. She shoved him away and fell against the cliff face. Sliding down, she curled up again. Her shoulders shook.

Peter touched his lip and checked for blood. The wind whistled.

Finally, Rosemary looked up. Her cheeks were wet. She took a rasping breath, and held it by biting her lip. She pressed against the rockface and levered herself up, ignoring Peter's helping hand. She stepped to the cliff and looked down. The wreckage below was still burning.

The wind shivered the fringe of her dress.

Finally, she cleared her nose with a sniff and drew herself up. "Let's go." She turned away from the devastation and limped to the bridge in her bare feet. Peter followed her. The smoke from the wreckage veiled them. Peter looked down. Rosemary didn't.

They trudged into darkness as the bridge met the tunnel. The click of scuffed stones echoed back at them. After several minutes, the light at the other end eased into view and a fresh breeze cut through the smell of damp soot.

Then their clothes changed.

Peter stumbled, then steadied himself on the tunnel wall. "Another story," he muttered. "I hope this is the last one."

He saw Rosemary in silhouette, in a jacket and a knee-length skirt, facing away from him. He stepped towards her. "Hey, are you —"

She turned suddenly and hugged him so hard, his breath left him.

"What was that for?" He held her.

"Promise me something?" she said, her voice muffled by his shirt front. "Stay close. Don't let me lose you like Puck."

"Look, you didn't —"

"Promise me!"

He hesitated. Then he laughed. "Stay close? They'd have to pull me off you."

They held each other a moment, then Rosemary pushed away. She walked down the tunnel faster than before.

As he followed, Peter shook his head and swallowed. There was a grip in his chest like fear. He could hear his heart beat. Then he realized it wasn't his heart but a deep rumble just beyond the edge of hearing. As they approached the exit, a new noise added itself: a regular hiss, easily mistaken for a gust of wind, but timed to that rumble that made the ground shiver beneath their feet.

Peter stopped. "What is that?"

Rosemary stopped and listened. Her shoulders tightened, then she stumbled forward. She reached the opening and stepped outside, staring, her arms limp in horror.

"Rosemary?" Peter started forward. "Rosemary, what is it?"

Rosemary stepped back unsteadily. She tripped on the rail and fell without a sound.

Peter caught up to her just as she was picking herself up. She didn't bat his hands away as he hauled her to her feet. He followed her wide-eyed gaze and almost let her go.

Before them, filling the bottom of a crater, stretched a white city. Chrome gleamed everywhere. The air was ozone and antiseptic. The buildings were square and alike and grouped like the rings of a tree, rising to a peak in the middle

Marble statues lined the edge of the crater, standing on podiums, each flanked by a pair of chrome jaguars like the ones they'd seen on the forest bridge.

And the sky was full of Zeppelins.

***

"I told you travelling at the speed of thought gets easier with practice!" said Marjorie.

She, Andrew, and John materialized, laughing. The laughter stopped when they looked around.

Marjorie gasped. "What is this place?"

***

"What is this place," Rosemary whispered.

"Rosemary?"

They were wearing jackets and white shirts. Rosemary was in a kilt; Peter in pressed pants. A school crest adorned their lapels. Rosemary looked down at her clothes, then yanked off her glasses. They had changed into horn-rims. She shook.

Peter pulled her to face him. "Come on, Rosemary, give! Where are we?"

"I can't do this, Peter," she gasped. "I can't! It's a horrible place."

"Look, the Zeppelins all came from here, so this must be the final challenge, right? We're almost finished with the story!"

"We're finished, all right."

"Rosemary!"

The voice was not Peter's. It drifted around them, indistinct, but Rosemary knew it at once.

She whirled around. "Theo!"

They were alone, yet Theo's voice echoed back from the edge of the crater. "Rosemary, no! Get out of here!"

"Theo, where are you?"

A girl's giggle rippled through the air. "That's enough talking," she said. "You just sit and wait for Rosemary."

"Rosemary?" said another voice, louder and more distinct. The nearest statue turned its head smoothly. Peter and Rosemary jumped.

"Rosemary Watson," said the statue. The voice issued from it as though from a speaker. "You have returned."

Peter and Rosemary stared nervously at the marble statue's blank eyes and hard face. It stood perfectly still.

"We have followed your quest to reach the city," the statue continued. "It was a wasted effort. The Zeppelins would have transported you."

"Yeah, as prisoners," said Peter.

Smooth as milk, the statue stepped down from the pedestal. "I am the forty-second Sentinel of the south-west quadrant. My function is to greet all who seek to enter the city and escort them to the Capital Centre. You will now come with me."

Peter swallowed. "Ah … thanks! Supposing we don't want to?"

The Sentinel's head twisted towards Peter. "That does not follow. You are here, therefore you must come with me."

Rosemary backed away. "No! I don't want to go! You can't make me!"

"If you cannot walk to the Capital Centre, we will find alternate means of transportation."

Peter touched her arm and nodded behind her. "Look."

She turned. Behind them, a Zeppelin lowered itself closer to the ground. A grapple dangled, flexing its fingers.

Rosemary closed her eyes. "I'll walk."

Gripping each other's hands, Peter and Rosemary walked down a flight of metal stairs that ran down the edge of the crater. The Sentinel came down behind, its stone feet clanking on the steps. The Zeppelin's shadow washed over them as they made their way through white streets.

The buildings grew higher the further they walked, until their feet echoed across marble canyons over the sound of the city's heart. Cars shaped like bullets hissed past without drivers. The shop window mannequins gleamed, but their clothes were bleached with time. Peter and Rosemary's reflections twisted in surfaces of chrome and moulded glass.

"What is this place?" asked Peter.

"The City," said the Sentinel.

"Does it have a name?"

"Yes. It is called The City."

Peter glanced sidelong at Rosemary. She was staring blankly ahead, lost in some memory. He nudged her. "What book was this?"

She started, then took a deep breath. "I don't remember the title. I read it two years ago. Don't you know?"

"I never read this book," said Peter. "Where are we? What happened? Where is everybody?"

* * *

"Is this where the people went?" asked Marjorie.

"Yes," said the Sentinel.

"That's comforting," deadpanned Andrew. "I think we should go now."

"Perhaps there was some disaster," said John. "I wonder what happened here; it's like the Marie Celeste!"

"Do you wish to see the people?" The Sentinel, moving stiffly on stone joints, stepped past them and pushed open the doors.

"That walking statue is just so creepy," said Andrew.

* * *

"Ours is a powerful civilization." The Sentinel cut into their thoughts. "We have built many wonders. But civilizations grow old, and old civilizations disappear. Knowing this, the people of this planet built the great Machine. The Machine was the pinnacle of our technology, capable of answering any question put to it and performing any action asked of it. We told it our fears and we asked it to preserve us so that our civilization would never die."

"The book I read," said Rosemary, "had three kids: a girl, her brother, and her friend. They came to this planet and found the same thing: the people had all vanished."

"What happened?" asked Peter.

"The Machine automated this planet and preserved the population for all eternity," said the Sentinel.

"Preserved? Preserved how?" asked Peter. "Where is everybody?"

They'd been following the street towards what they thought was a white wall. Suddenly the buildings around them fell away and they entered a huge plaza. All the streets in the city radiated out like strands in a web. At the centre was a building as tall as a searchlight, one great column fluted with lines of chrome. White steps led up towards large doors cut into the sides.

Peter goggled. "Whoa." Rosemary stood silent, her face as white as the flagstones.

"The people are here," said the Sentinel.

"That's nice," croaked Peter. "Can we go now?"

"No." The Sentinel suddenly clamped its hands around the scruffs of their necks. Peter and Rosemary cried out. Rosemary's knees buckled and she scrabbled at the stone fingers, but the Sentinel held on tight. "You must complete your journey. You must meet the people." He marched them across the plaza, their feet barely touching the flagstones, and mounted the stairs.

Peter struggled to move his legs fast enough to keep from bruising his shins. "Let go of me! Let go!"

"No, please," gasped Rosemary. "Don't take me in there!"

The marble doors swung open as they approached, flanked by chrome jaguars. The cold darkness swallowed them and the doors slammed shut behind them. The Sentinel dropped them onto a black floor inside a hall that reverberated with the heartbeat of the city.

Rubbing the back of his neck, Peter picked himself up. "We could have walked, you know," he snapped. He looked for Rosemary and found her lying on the floor, limp as a rag doll.

She shook off his helping hand and picked herself up. Her eyes stayed fixed on the floor like someone condemned. "Don't look, Peter," she whispered. "Don't look at the slabs."

"Slabs?" He looked. Around them, blocks of marble hung from the ceiling, like double doors only thicker. Row upon row stretched out before them. Some swayed, as if something inside them stirred. "What are —"

"I'll go!" Rosemary snapped, shrugging off the prodding hand of the Sentinel. She stepped forward down the aisle between the slabs. Peter followed. He could see the stones front on now. His eyes widened.

"Oh."

Embedded in each slab was the representation of a person, arms folded across chest, mouth open in a last gasp, blank eyes staring. There were hundreds of slabs on either side of them and the aisle stretched into the distance, with at least a hundred slabs ahead of them. Each bore a representation of a person, their skin and clothes white like the marble, but each one as different as one living person is from another.

Peter swallowed. "This is it. These are the people, aren't they? They're tombstones! The Machine turned everybody into stone!"

The Sentinel nudged them onto a moving walkway that sped them past the slabs. "Some had concerns, but the Machine soon convinced all that its solution was the best. And how could it not? Here in the Hall of Stability, our civilization no longer fears death."

Peter caught sight of a little girl in a pressed dress, holding a doll clasped to her chest. He turned away.

"Oh my God!"

"I'm sorry, Peter," whispered Rosemary. "I should never have brought you here."

"Don't," Peter snapped. He kept his eyes on the floor. "Don't say that."

They stumbled off the moving sidewalk and looked up. Cathedral doors of chrome stood at the centre of an obsidian wall. Flanking the doorway were the characters. Rosemary swallowed. "This is it."

Peter clasped her hand and squeezed. "Yeah."

Two of the characters, a butler with the red impression of a noose around his neck and a girl in her late teens wearing a leather jacket covered in badges, her skin blue from asphyxiation, turned and pushed open the doors. The mechanical beat intensified, catching at their hearts and their breathing. They entered. The characters filed in after them.

Waiting at the end of the hall was the Machine.

The Machine was a volcanic upwelling of chrome and stainless steel. There were no controls. A huge mechanical arm stretched up and was lost somewhere in the darkness, rising and falling with the regularity of an oil pump.

Peter leaned close. "Rosemary, the book, what happened to the kids?"

* * *

There was the sound of clanging metal, the hiss of steam. Her brother's yells ended abruptly.

"Andrew! John!" Marjorie screamed. She struggled vainly against the metal cables wrapping around her body, pulling her to the Machine. "No!"

***

Rosemary flinched.

"Rosemary, what happened in the book?" asked Peter.

"They were turned to stone," said Rosemary quietly.

Peter went white. "All of them?"

"The Machine took Andrew and John," said Rosemary. "Marjorie screamed …"

"And then?"

"Yes, Rosemary," said a girl's clear voice. "And then?"

The girl with the horn-rimmed glasses stood at the top of a flight of stairs leading up to the Machine. She was dressed in a school uniform like Rosemary's. A chrome jaguar nuzzled her as she scratched it behind its ears. In her other hand she held a tablet of paper.

Rosemary swallowed hard. "Marjorie. Marjorie Campbell."

"Rosemary Watson," said Marjorie. The sandpaper harshness of her voice was gone. Her words rang through the chamber, a clear soprano.

She smiled. "Welcome to the Machine."

Chapter Twelve

M arjorie began to clap, slowly and deliberately, as she came down the steps. "Bravo, Rosemary," she said. "Bravo! That was an action-filled adventure such as I have rarely read. You are definite hero material, and Peter is an excellent sidekick."

"Hey!" said Peter.

Marjorie smirked. "It's a pity it will all end in tears."

Rosemary faced Marjorie. "Where's Theo?"

Marjorie shrugged. "Exactly where I left him, I should think, and perfectly preserved for the occasion."

Rosemary's eyes widened. "No! You didn't —"

Marjorie climbed the stairs to the Machine and walked around beside it. Suspended to the left by cables was something draped with white cloth. Marjorie pulled the cloth away, revealing a slab with

Theo embedded in it. His skin and his clothes were as white as the marble around him. His arms were folded across his chest. No life lit his eyes.

Rosemary staggered. Peter held her. "Let him go!" she yelled. "He didn't do anything to you!"

Marjorie shrugged. "He was your brother. That was enough."

"Enough for what?" Rosemary shook herself free of Peter's grip. "What do you want from me?"

"I also had an older brother," said Marjorie. Her gaze shifted towards Peter. "I also had a friend."

Rosemary whirled around. "No!"

Metal claws swooped in and grabbed Peter's ankles and wrists. He yelled as more wires wrapped around him and pulled him towards the Machine.

"Peter!" Rosemary rushed forward, but two characters caught her by the arms. She stamped her heel on a foot and jabbed her elbow into a stomach. They let go. She grabbed Peter and strained, digging in her heels, but she was no match for the Machine's strength. Her feet slid on the polished floor.

Then someone grabbed her from behind, prying her arms loose. She screamed and struggled, but Peter slipped free. A thick arm in a wet wool sleeve wrapped over her throat. She choked. Peter was wrenched into the air and lowered onto a marble slab at the base of the Machine.

The slab rose on a hoist. Meeting it halfway from the ceiling was a metal press. The press and the hoist came together. There was the clang of machinery, the hiss of steam. Peter's yells stopped.

Rosemary's scream ended in a sob. She sagged into the character's restraining arm. Behind her, Marjorie giggled. "Now you really are alone." Her laughter echoed over the heartbeat of the Machine.

The character holding her, the tall man in the long, wet tweed coat and deerstalker hat, swung Rosemary around and threw her at Marjorie's feet.

Marjorie smiled. "Your turn."

Metal claws whipped down and grabbed Rosemary's wrists and ankles, folding her arms across her chest. More wires wrapped around her, and more. Wires wrapped around her mouth, cutting off her screams. The bonds wrapped her tighter than Peter had been wrapped, until she was almost a metal mummy.

Then her right arm burst through the wires as though they were made of paper.

Marjorie swore under her breath. Rosemary stared at her arm. The rest of her body was bound so tight, she couldn't move, but the wires wrapping around her right arm couldn't hold it. It had survived the grip of a huge metal grapple without a scratch, and it was still black from the Sea of Ink.

Rosemary grabbed at the wires around her mouth. They broke against her fingers, and she spat out strands of metal. She tore at her other bonds, and then punched Marjorie as the girl rushed her.

Marjorie went sliding back along the marble floor, clutching her chin. Rosemary pulled herself free of the last of the strands.

Marjorie sat up, flexing her jaw. "Cursed hero luck!" she muttered. "But I guess it wouldn't be a climax without a battle." She stood and presented her tablet like a sword. "I have the most powerful weapon in all of fiction: a pad of paper and a pencil. You have residue from the Sea of Ink as your shield, no weapon. How long do you think you can hold out, Rosemary?"

One by one, the characters folded from sight, leaving Rosemary alone with Marjorie. The two girls stared at each other. Behind them, the Machine beat away.

Then Marjorie opened her tablet and scribbled something. A laser pistol appeared on the paper. She grabbed it up and aimed.

Rosemary ran.

The laser beams kicked up sparks and smoke at Rosemary's heels as she dashed for the cover of an alcove. Instinct made her drop and roll and a beam seared overhead. Then she was inside.

The alcove was a doorway, leading to a narrow hallway paralleling the Hall of the Machine.

Rosemary stumbled to her feet and ran.

A samurai emerged from the shadows, swinging at her with a kendo stick. Rosemary brought up her right arm to shield herself. The cane snapped in half, but Rosemary barely flinched. Out of the corner of her eye, she saw the black mark shrink on her arm as the blow hit, like a pen draining away.

Rosemary punched. Her left hand had little effect on the leather armour, but her right knocked the samurai aside. She ran on.

"Go ahead, Rosemary, run." Marjorie's voice echoed through the marble halls. "Run away as you always do. Leave me here, again."

At a junction, a scientist wearing a tattered white coat, his skin pockmarked from dozens of gigantic insect bites, held up a ray gun. Rosemary grabbed the corner and swung herself into the corridor. A jagged beam of electricity missed her by inches.

"But wait," echoed Marjorie's voice. "You can't run away this time, can you? You're trapped in this place, on the page."

Rosemary tripped on a wire strung out along the hall and pulled tight by two frozen young children. They pounced on her, kicking and jumping on her back. She turned, shielding her face with her arms. The black ink seeped down her arm with every blow. She struggled back to her feet and kept running.

"That's the problem with being the hero, Rosemary," shouted Marjorie. "You might be able to escape this place, but you won't. You wouldn't dream of leaving Peter and Theo behind. *My* brother and friend, maybe, but not yours."

Rosemary reached the end of the corridor and threw open the door. The Hall of Stability stretched out before her. It was a clear run from there to the outside.

The door clicked shut behind her, but Rosemary didn't move. She stood there, breathing heavily. She leaned against the door and covered her face with her hands.

Marjorie's voice was a distant echo. "I *told* you you couldn't leave."

Rosemary looked up. Through the gaps in her fingers, she could see the marble slabs, row upon row, swaying in the disturbed air.

She lowered her hands and took a deep breath. "You're right," she muttered. "I can't leave. What sort of person would I be if I could?"

She turned around and opened the door she'd just stepped through. There she stopped dead.

The hallway was filled with characters.

They streamed out after her as she ran. She tried to cross the Hall of Stability to the main door that had taken them to the Hall of the Machine, but in the open they caught her. Yelling, she flailed blindly. But for every character Rosemary knocked aside, another stepped forward.

She struggled through them and ran.

The man in the deerstalker hat barred her way. She swung a punch, but gasped as she found her hand caught in his strong grip. Her right arm was now as pink as her left.

He pulled Rosemary forward, twisting her arm painfully behind her back. "You seem to have run out of ink, my dear!" The damp of his clothes seeped through to her back. He gave her arm another twist to make her squeak.

They carried her into the Hall of the Machine and tossed her back at Marjorie's feet.

"You're trapped here, Rosemary," said Marjorie, vanishing her laser pistol back into the tablet. "The hero has no choice but to come back."

Rosemary shot up onto her hands and knees. Her breathing quickened. Her eyes glistened. "The hero always wins!" And with a yell, she made a mad dash at Marjorie.

Marjorie caught her and twisted her arm behind her. They both faced the Machine. "Not always," Marjorie whispered. "And never without sacrifice."

Rosemary looked up. Suspended in mid-air opposite Theo was Peter.

Rosemary sank to her knees.

Marjorie stood behind her, tapping her pencil against her lips. "You know, now that we have you, I don't know what to do with you. What should I do with you, Rosemary? Should we borrow a few pages from H.P. Lovecraft, perhaps? Or maybe Edgar Allen Poe? Or should I just leave you to the Machine?"

"Stop it!" Rosemary sobbed, whirling around. "Stop it, please! Let Peter and Theo go! Please! I didn't do anything to you!"

The characters began to whisper.

Marjorie shook her head in disbelief. "Didn't do anything to us?! You —" She sputtered, then took a deep breath. Her pencil snapped in half. "All of you! Show Rosemary why you're here!"

The characters closed in.

Rosemary stumbled to her feet.

The man in the deerstalker hat strode out of the darkness, his clothes dripping. "You left me as I went over the falls."

A scream echoed in Rosemary's head, wailing and fading into the distance, until it was lost in the rumbling of the cataract. Rosemary turned away.

A Second World War fighter pilot stepped forward. "The plane fell apart around me. You weren't there!"

Rosemary heard the roar of straining engines, the crackle of fire. She could see the ground rushing up at her face. She flinched and staggered.

Marjorie watched, her arms folded across her chest.

The insect-bitten scientist stared at her with haunted eyes. "You left me with them! THEM!"

Two men wearing hard hats with lanterns, their faces black with coal dust, stepped forward. "The air was running out," said one.

"Who's going to feed my family?" said the other.

Choking on bad air, Rosemary turned again and stopped dead. Lydia stepped forward, blood on her face. "The house had me. The Beast broke through the door. Where were you?"

Snarls. Screams. A surge of boiling darkness.

Rosemary turned again and faced a woman in a spacesuit, holding a smoking blaster. "The alien killed everyone on board my ship. I'm the only one left."

They were closing in, surrounding her, leaving one escape route open, a doorway. Rosemary ran for it, brushing past Marjorie, rushed through.

Marjorie wrote something on her tablet of paper. She smiled.

In the corridor, Rosemary let out a horrible, pro-longed scream. Then there was silence.

CHAPTER THIRTEEN
THE THREE OUT OF THE FOUR

"It was the worst moment of my life.
And that's when you stopped reading!"
— Marjorie Campbell

There was silence in the Hall of the Machine. One by one, the characters folded out of existence, leaving Marjorie alone. She stood a moment, staring at the door through which Rosemary had run, then closed her tablet of paper, pocketed her pencil, and followed.

Rosemary was sprawled in mid-air, caught in a spider's web with strands as thick as her fingers stretched between the black marble walls. New strands drifted over her shoulders like a shawl and tightened.

Marjorie sidled around the web, pushed her glasses further up on her nose, and glanced at her notes. "The spiders that made this web have been known to keep their victims alive for days, going so far as to forcefeed them." She clicked her tongue. "The things kids read nowadays."

"You can't leave me here," Rosemary croaked.

"Why not?" Marjorie snapped her tablet closed. "Wouldn't it be justice?" She turned on her heel and began to walk away down the corridor.

Rosemary's mind raced. If Marjorie left, it was all over. She had to make her stay! Had to!

"Marjorie!" Her voice echoed. "Wait!"

"Goodbye, Rosemary!" Marjorie's footsteps faded into the distance.

Wait, thought Rosemary. *Weren't villains supposed to stay and gloat?*

"Marjorie, please, just tell me why you're doing this!"

The distant footsteps stopped. Rosemary's heart thumped. She blew at a strand of web that fell across her cheek and tried to ignore the rustling sound coming from by her ear.

Marjorie hesitated, took a couple of steps, then the corridor echoed to her approach. Rosemary could only gaze at the black and white checkerboard floor until Marjorie stepped into her field of vision, her shoulders stiff.

Rosemary licked her lips and looked her in the eye. "Just spell it out for me. You know you want to."

Marjorie's jaw clenched. "You abandoned me."

"What? Marjorie, no! I'd never —"

"When you stopped reading my book, you abandoned me!" Marjorie snapped. She turned away.

Rosemary strained against the web. "But I don't understand —"

Marjorie rounded on her. "You left me at my worst moment! I'd lost everything to the Machine: my brother, my friend. And just when I was about to lose myself, you stoppped reading!"

"But I didn't leave you!" Rosemary gulped. "I was there! Y-you screamed and screamed! I — I had to do something! I thought if I stopped reading, I could stop it from happening!"

"You ran away!" There was a world of contempt in Marjorie's voice. "Do you know what happens when the story stops? Imagine what it's like when everything's against you, and it keeps getting worse! Imagine what it's like when life and death come down to a single choice in a single moment. Then imagine that when that moment comes ... everything stops."

Marjorie struggled to get her breathing under control. She couldn't. Her voice rose in pitch. "And you're trapped. Trapped in the worst moment of your life, with release so close but coming no closer. Can you imagine that? Can you, dear reader? *Can you*?"

Her last words came as a shriek. She reared back and slapped Rosemary hard across the face. The web shook. Rosemary looked back at her, agape.

Sobbing, Marjorie struck out again and again. Then she tore Rosemary from the web, threw her to the floor, and straddled her, slapping and punching. "You left me to the Machine! You left me to die! You abandoned me! I hate you!" Tears streamed down her cheeks.

Shielding herself, Rosemary struggled up and threw her arms around Marjorie as the girl collapsed, crying, onto Rosemary's shoulder.

"You left me to die!" Marjorie choked, giving Rosemary's back a last half-hearted thump. Then she sagged into Rosemary's arms.

"But I don't understand," said Rosemary after Marjorie's sobs ebbed. "What if I finished reading and you really were turned to stone?"

"Then she would have met her destiny," said a voice around her. "She would be at peace. She would not be suspended in mid-air."

Rosemary looked around in delighted astonishment. "Puck! You're alive! How?"

"Fictional characters never really die," said Puck. He appeared before Rosemary, holding a book open to the end. He flipped the pages to the front. "One need only turn to the beginning of the book, and they live again."

Marjorie pushed away from Rosemary and rounded on Puck, raising her hands as though to call up a spell. Puck raised his hands, palms out. "Truce," he said. "I think Rosemary has something to say to you."

Marjorie turned to Rosemary. Rosemary swallowed hard and brushed a stray strand of web from her hair.

"I'm sorry."

"Sorry?" Marjorie exclaimed. "Sorry?!"

"I know it's not enough," Rosemary cut in, "but it's a start. I didn't know how you felt. All I saw was someone hurting, and I couldn't stand it. I wouldn't have left you if I knew how you felt. Let Theo and Peter go, and I'll do what you want."

"Why should I trust you?" said Marjorie.

"You're the one who has control of the Machine," said Rosemary. "You're the one who has dozens of heroes on her side. You have all the power. What have you got to lose? Or is revenge all you want?"

Marjorie thought for a moment. "I accept," she said. She opened her notebook and crossed something out.

Peter and Theo materialized in the corridor in front of them. They looked at each other, then down at themselves. Then Theo, seeing his sister, cried "Rosemary!" as he rushed forward and hugged her, swinging her in the air.

"I knew you could do it, Rosemary!" Peter cried. He rounded on Marjorie. "We have you now! You'd better surrender!"

"Peter," said Rosemary, struggling out of Theo's embrace and pulling Peter back by his shoulder. "Um, Peter? She won."

Peter and Theo stared at her.

Theo stepped forward. "What do you mean, she won?"

Rosemary turned to Marjorie, who stood, arms folded, pencil clasped tight. "Look, all of this was because I gave up, right? I didn't know what I was doing then. I know now. Let Peter and Theo go and give me a second chance. I promise, I won't let you down."

The frown faded from Marjorie's face. She blinked at Rosemary.

"What are you talking about?" said Peter.

But Rosemary kept her focus on Marjorie. "Let me finish your story with you."

"What?" shouted Theo.

Marjorie gaped. "You would do that? After all I've done to you?"

"Think carefully what you are saying, Sage Rosemary," said Puck, his face grim. "We are inside Marjorie's book. You would not be reading the story but improvising its end. You would be thrust into Marjorie's place and expected to live or die, not according to the plot, but by your wits alone."

"How is that different from what I've been doing since we got here?" said Rosemary.

"If you expect a happy ending, do not do so," said Puck. "There is no telling what the end might be. If it is not a happy one, you could be trapped in Marjorie's story, as lost in the outside world as Theo was."

"But Theo will be free, won't he?" asked Rosemary.

"If you go through with this, yes," said Marjorie.

"His life in exchange for mine?" Rosemary took a deep breath. "Fair enough."

"No!" Theo and Peter sprang forward. Theo grabbed Rosemary by the shoulders. "Rosie, don't do this."

She flinched. "I have to."

"No, you don't!" He shook her. "Not after all she's done! You're not giving yourself up to her!"

"Theo," Rosemary gasped. "You're hurting me."

"Why do we have to play by their rules?" he shouted. "She's just a book. She's just words on the page. She has no power over us if we don't let her."

"Theo, don't you understand?" Rosemary shook herself from his grip. "Marjorie isn't fiction. Marjorie is me."

Peter gaped. "What?"

"All these characters," said Rosemary. "I was so afraid they'd get hurt. Don't you see? I'm always afraid that I'll get hurt. That's why I'm alone at school. I keep saying I don't have an imagination, but I'm wrong, we're standing in it. I've got to face my fears!"

"What fears?" said Theo. "What would make you think this way?"

"Because bad things happened to others I loved," said Rosemary.

Silence hung in the air. Then Theo turned away.

Rosemary turned to Marjorie. "Look at you. I knew I was looking in a mirror the first time I saw you." She grinned. "I loved travelling with you, Andrew, and John at the speed of thought."

Marjorie smiled. "Do you remember the planet of negative dimensions?"

"You didn't like that at first. Left was right and in was out."

"We got used to it," said Marjorie.

"And then you jumped again, and ended up in the city of the Machine." Rosemary's smile disappeared. "And then I left you. I shouldn't have. I've got to see you through to the end."

Marjorie's eyes shifted down from Rosemary's gaze.

Rosemary stepped back. "Let Peter and Theo out of here and I'll finish what I started."

Marjorie didn't look up. "Deal."

"When do we start?"

"Whenever you are ready. You should say your goodbyes."

Rosemary turned to Puck. "Can't you come with me?"

Puck smiled sadly. "I am no hero, Sage Rosemary, I was merely your guide, and I have brought you to your goal. The rest is up to you."

She hugged him. "I liked your story most of all."

Then she turned to Theo and touched his shoulder. He faced her. "Why are you doing this, Rosie?"

"Because you're my brother. You've gotten me out of trouble more times than I can count."

"That's my job," he said. "To take care of my little sister. It doesn't work the other way."

"It does, sometimes." She hugged him. "I love you."

He held her. "I love you too, little Sage."

She pulled away at last. "I have to go." She turned to Peter. He grinned nervously and held out his hand.

He grunted when Rosemary hugged him, clasping him close, pushing the air from his lungs. He held her for a second, until they pulled apart quickly. Rosemary shifted on her feet and clasped her hands behind her. "Thanks," she said.

"Don't mention it," he replied, looking at the floor.

She stepped back to Marjorie and took her hand. "Goodbye," she said to everyone. To Marjorie she said, "Ready?" The other girl nodded.

"No." Theo started forward. "Rosemary, I can't let you do this!"

"Now!" said Marjorie.

Rosemary closed her eyes and concentrated. The two girls disappeared.

CHAPTER FOURTEEN

WELCOME TO THE MACHINE

"It has to be me. There is no one else."
— Rosemary Watson

Peter struggled out from darkness, as though from a bad dream. "Rosemary!" he cried.

Hands grabbed his flailing wrists. "Easy, son, easy." Mr. Watson soothed him. "You're out of there. You're all right."

Peter glanced around the living room. Trisha sat on the couch, silent and pale. Mrs. Watson was holding down her son. "Theo, it's okay! You're back now!"

"But she's still in there," Theo sobbed. "She —"

Peter's gaze shot to the corner. Rosemary sat, propped against the wall, surrounded by pillows, her chin to her chest, her eyes closed. He shot forward. "Rosemary!"

"There's nothing you can do!" Mr. Watson pulled him back. "We read everything. We know what's going on."

Peter blinked. They'd read everything? How? He turned. "The book!"

They rushed over to the coffee table. Flipping the book open to its last page of text, they began to read.

When Rosemary opened her eyes, she saw that she was standing on the embankment where she had first seen the automated city. The empty buildings stretched out before her, cresting in the distance into the towers that housed the Machine.

How did I get out here? she thought. Then she realized. Before succumbing to the Machine, Marjorie must have transported away at the speed of thought. But she couldn't leave Andrew and John behind, so she would come back.

Marjorie stood beside her. She swallowed hard. Then she looked at Rosemary. For a moment, the two girls faced each other in silence.

Rosemary took a deep breath and walked towards Marjorie. Marjorie walked towards Rosemary. They met like two sides of a mirror, and then Rosemary turned and faced the city, looking through Marjorie's eyes. Taking another deep breath, Rosemary/Marjorie struck out for the city.

One of the Sentinels followed her as she made her way down the metal steps at the rim of the crater. She ignored it. She ran over in her mind what she had to do.

I have to rescue Andrew and John. But how? I'm just a girl. ("Two girls," said someone sharply inside her brain.) *How can I take on a machine?*

It has to be me. There is no one else.

Even realizing this, her feet dragged as she walked through the city towards the building of the Machine. The Sentinel did not prod her forward. She trudged along steadily, step by slow step.

Then she looked up and saw that she was at the entrance to the great building in the centre of the city. No matter how slowly she had walked, her footsteps had taken her here. Rosemary/Marjorie squared her shoulders and mounted the steps. The Sentinel pushed open the huge marble doors for her, but she didn't say a word. She trudged through the Hall of Stability, keeping her eyes on the ground. The doors to the Hall of the Machine opened before her.

The slow beat of the Machine resonated in her chest, catching at her breathing again, punching through her concentration and quickening her steps to its rhythm. Before she knew it, she had been pushed up the steps and was six feet away. She stared up at it.

"You have returned," said a voice projected from the Machine, deep as a tectonic plate. "You have come to accept the inevitable."

"No," said Marjorie, her voice sounding small and feeble in her ears. "I've come to set my brother and my friend free. Please, let them go."

"That is not my function," said the Machine.

"We stumbled on your planet by accident. We wouldn't have come here if we knew what would happen. We don't belong here. Let us go!"

"That is not my function."

"How do you expect people to remember your civilization if you turn all your visitors into stone?" demanded Marjorie. "Please! It's my fault we came here! I just wanted to see interesting things. Show some mercy!"

"That is not my function," said the Machine. "My function is to preserve this planet. Everyone on this planet must survive. You are on this planet, and so you will survive."

Metal claws reached out from nowhere and grabbed her wrists and ankles.

"I give you immortality."

Rosemary/Marjorie screamed.

"Let me end your suffering. Give your troubles to me. Welcome to the Machine."

The claws pulled her down and laid her prone on a marble slab at the base of the Machine, arms folded across her chest. The slab began to rise into the air. Other metal pinions wrapped around her, holding her head steady, pressing the backs of her legs to the marble. Steam hissed and metal clanged all around her.

Rosemary/Marjorie struggled, but the metal bonds held her fast. Her eyes tracked up and she saw a metal slab, descending fast.

Her scream was cut off by the clang of metal against metal and a hiss of steam.

All was black. She couldn't move.

I'm flattened, thought Marjorie. *But how can I still be alive if I've been flattened? I can't feel my heartbeat. I can't breathe. I don't feel the need to breathe. Am I dead? But why am I still here?*

A moment later, the metal press pulled away. Rosemary/Marjorie stared after it; she could do nothing but stare after it. Her eyes wouldn't move. She could see her reflection in the metal of the press. Her body and her clothes were white. She was part of the marble.

Grapples descended. They hoisted the slab into the air and carried it through the Hall of the Machine. The windows and the detail of the walls passed in front of her vision, followed by the blank faces of the stone slabs as she entered the Hall of Stability.

They placed her by the wall at the end of the hall. The grapples left, and silence fell.

She tried to move, but there was no part of her that she could move. Not even the sound of her blood rushed in her ears.

Oh my God! Her thoughts bounced through her head. *I'll be like this forever. Fixed in place forever! What can I do if my heart won't even beat?*

Her gaze was fixed forward. It fell upon two stone slabs, one holding a boy her age, the other an older teenager.

Andrew and John. Of course, they were the last to be processed. The Machine would place them together at the end of the hall and her along with them.

Andrew! she cried out silently. *John! What do I do? What do we do? It can't end like this! It can't!*

Then she heard a whisper in her head.

"Quiet your thoughts," said the Machine. "You are disturbing the sleep of others around you."

Others can hear me? thought Marjorie.

She listened. After a while, below the surface of sound, she could hear whispering as though through a closed door.

Who's there? her thought went out. *Can somebody help me? Can somebody get me out?*

Get us out! came a voice at the edge of conscious thought. Other voices murmured in agreement.

The voice of the Machine grew dark. "You are here now. You have been preserved. So you shall remain for all eternity. Nothing you can do will change that."

I can't move! a thought protested.

Let me out! thought another. *I'm going crazy! I want out!*

"Quiet your thoughts," said the Machine. "You cannot get out. You have been preserved for so long that to free you would turn you to dust. I am the only thing between your civilization and dust."

What about me? thought Marjorie. *What about Andrew and John? We only arrived yesterday.*

The Machine did not answer for a moment. Finally it said, "You cannot get out."

I can be free, thought Marjorie. *You wouldn't try to talk me out of trying if there wasn't any hope of it. There's still hope for me, and for Andrew and John. We can be free! I want us to be free!*

"What hope do you have?" whispered the voice of the Machine. "Quiet your thoughts. Cease your struggle."

I want to be free! thought Marjorie.

"You have no hope."

I want to be free!

"You cannot get out."

I want to be free!

"Escape is impossible."

Nothing is impossible, thought Rosemary, her thoughts cutting across Marjorie's panic. *I thought saving Theo was impossible, but it happened. It was the sixth impossible thing I gave to the Ferryman. Anything can happen in the Land of Fiction. Perhaps I can get out of this. Please, God, I hope I can get out of this!*

Hope warmed her heart, and at that moment, Rosemary/Marjorie's heart began to beat.

It was painful, at first. The flesh struck against her stone lungs, and she couldn't even draw breath to cry out, but gradually warmth spread through her chest, as the stone softened and turned back to flesh. The white of Rosemary/Marjorie's cheeks flushed slowly to pink.

Her throat cleared and she pulled in her first breath with a gasp. Pupils reappeared in her eyes, and she could blink tears into them.

Her skin regained its pink, her clothes their bright colours. She broke from the stone that held her in place. Her muscles stiff, she fell onto the floor.

Marjorie got up, separating from Rosemary, and ran to the slabs holding her brother and her friend.

"Andrew! John!" she cried. "I made it out! You have to hope!" She jumped up and down into their field of vision. "The Machine takes away all hope. You have to hope to get free. Andrew, John, look at me! I'm free. You can be free too, just as long as you keep hope!"

Pink began to touch Andrew's checks. The pupils reappeared in John's eyes. Marjorie danced in relief.

Then Andrew and John fell from their slabs and lay limp on the floor. Marjorie rushed over to them. Soon they were on their feet, babbling and hugging each other.

A sigh rushed through the Hall of Stability. Far away, the Machine groaned. Cracks appeared in the walls and leapt and jumped across the floors and ceilings. Cracks appeared in the slabs around them and the stones started to crumble to dust. Rosemary was sure she saw one man smile and wink at her before he disappeared.

"You saved us, Marjorie!" John cried.

Andrew pushed them away from a stream of falling stone. "We've got to get out of here."

"You two go. I'll follow you."

The two boys hesitated, but one look at Marjorie made them step back and concentrate. They disappeared from the planet.

Marjorie turned and helped Rosemary to her feet.

"Thank you," said Marjorie, all trace of malice gone from her voice. "I think you saved me in more ways than one."

Rosemary smiled. "You're welcome."

"I didn't like playing the villain," said Marjorie. "All that hate and anger." She shuddered.

"You would have lost, too." Rosemary's voice was light. "The villains always lose."

"Not always."

"But sometimes. Life's full of happy endings."

"Listen ..." Marjorie faltered, her smile sheepish and nervous. "I know I haven't given you any reason to help me, but ... I only just met Andrew, and ... well, he's nice and ..." She gave Rosemary a shy smile. "I think there's a sequel."

Rosemary hugged her. "I'll read it. I promise."

Marjorie stepped back. With a final smile, she concentrated, and then vanished.

The floor began to shake. Rosemary ducked as a piece of masonry fell. Gaps appeared in the walls and she could see the sky. It seemed to be on fire. "Um ... Can somebody give me instructions on how to travel at the speed of thought? Hello?"

The shaking intensified. The rising dust began to claw at her lungs. She coughed.

Then Puck appeared before her, smiling broadly even as the columns collapsed.

He took her hand and together they ran through the Hall of Stability, leaping nimbly over the fallen stones. Outside, a thousand *Hindenburg*s fell from the sky.

Puck turned into an eagle. Holding onto his wing as she had his hand, Rosemary felt herself soaring up into the air. Beneath her, the city of marble and chrome was crumbling into dust.

A part of her thought that this wasn't right. She was barely touching Puck's wing. It was though she were rising in the air currents by herself. She looked at Puck.

"Do not question," he said. "Enjoy."

They rose higher and higher, until the sky lost its blue and turned black, and stars came out. The air thinned. Rosemary was dizzy, but she didn't care. Blackness was creeping into her vision, but instead of falling unconscious, she felt as though she were waking up.

Puck's voice whispered in her ear. "Farewell, my brave Sage Rosemary."

Rosemary opened her eyes. She was in her living room, surrounded by pillows. Her family were around her, cheering.

Theo enveloped her in a tight hug. "Rosie, you saved me!"

Rosemary's mother hugged them both. "You did it!"

"You made it out!" exclaimed Peter. "Rosemary, I don't —" He cut himself off. Then, smiling to himself, he slipped out of the throng to the front door, pulled on his boots and coat, and slipped outside.

Trisha was bouncing up and down and hugging everybody she could. "My sister's a hero!"

Tears ran down Rosemary's cheeks. "I'm sorry, Mom! I'm sorry, Theo! It was all my fault."

"Don't you dare say that," said Mrs. Watson. "You're okay now, and that's all that matters."

Rosemary looked at Theo. "A happy ending!" She hugged him.

Theo squeezed her.

Then it was a flurry of more hugs and thank yous and Shamus licking Rosemary's face …

Suddenly, Rosemary frowned. "Where's Peter?"

They looked around. Peter was gone.

Rosemary jumped up and ran to the front door. She darted outside.

Peter was in his boots and jacket. He was trudging down the front walk.

"Wait!" called Rosemary, standing on the porch. Peter stopped. After a moment, he turned. He stood with his hands in his pockets.

Rosemary came down the porch steps and walked up to him. They stood staring at each other, breath fogging. The silence lengthened uncomfortably. Then, both at once, they hugged each other.

"Thank you," said Rosemary at last.

"Any time," said Peter. "Well, not any time. I don't want to do that again, but —"

She cut him off. "Listen. Have you got plans this Christmas?"

Peter shrugged. "My uncle's buying a special turkey TV dinner."

Rosemary laughed. She looked at him. "How does a *real* turkey dinner sound? My parents always have a big dinner on Christmas Day. Perhaps you and your uncle can come along, around five?"

"Did your parents say it was okay?"

"They will. I'll make sure of that."

Peter smiled uncertainly.

The silence stretched uncomfortably again.

"I'd better get back in," said Rosemary. "It's freezing."

"I'll see you later, Sage."

"Just don't call me that in front of anybody else."

They hugged once more, and then Peter turned and trudged up the country road.

As Rosemary watched him go, she muttered, "I wonder what the next book brings." She smiled and went inside. The living room was empty. Everybody was in the kitchen, preparing a feast of celebration.

"I'm just going up to my room," Rosemary called out. She paused by the fiction shelves in the living room and pulled out a book. Then she slipped upstairs and lay on her bed.

She looked at the cover. It showed Marjorie and Andrew creeping up towards a scary old house. Their expressions were nervous, but determined.

Rosemary opened the book, and then frowned and looked at her right palm. There was a stain in the centre of it, like a birthmark, but bluc-black like the ink from the sea. It hadn't been there before. She rubbed at it, but it wouldn't come off.

Maybe it would never come off.

She shrugged and returned to her book.